RITS

Mariken Jongman

TRANSLATED FROM THE DUTCH BY

Wanda Boeke

Front Street
Asheville, North Carolina

Publication has been made possible with financial support from the Foundation for the Production and Translation of Dutch Literature.

Text copyright © 2005 by Mariken Jongman
English translation copyright © 2008 by Wanda Boeke
All rights reserved
Printed in the United States of America
Designed by Helen Robinson
First U.S. edition, 2008

LIBRARY OF CONGRESS CATALOGING-IN-PUBLICATION DATA
Jongman, Mariken.
  Rits / by Mariken Jongman;
translated from the Dutch by Wanda J. Boeke.—
1st U.S. ed.
  p. cm.
Summary: When his father runs off with his girlfriend
and his distraught mother is admitted to an institution,
thirteen-year-old Rits goes to live with his uncle and
tries to make the best of his unusual circumstances.
ISBN 978-1-59078-545-4 (hardcover : alk. paper)
[1. Uncles—Fiction. 2. Family problems—Fiction.
3. Friendship—Fiction.]
I. Boeke, Wanda. II. Title.
PZ7.J74155Ri 2008
[Fic]—dc22
                                     2007021596

FRONT STREET
An Imprint of Boyds Mills Press, Inc.
815 Church Street
Honesdale, Pennsylvania 18431

RITS

Monday, July 4

For my birthday last year, my parents got me a writing journal and pen and a video camera. That way I could still choose what I wanted to be, a writer or a filmmaker.

"But what if I happen to want to be something else?" I asked.

"Like what?" asked my mom.

"I don't know," I said. "Maybe something at a post office." That would be cool, I thought, sitting at a counter window and doing all kinds of things.

"Well, have fun." (By the look on her face, I don't think she meant it.)

She also said one time that if I wanted to be a writer or a film-maker someday, I'd better start now. She had looked at me with concern and asked, Wasn't my childhood *too* happy?

"How do you mean?" I wanted to know.

Here it comes. She said, "It's handy for artists to have had an unhappy childhood."

I had no idea what she meant.

My mom laughed. "Just a joke," she said.

At the time, I didn't think twice about it, but now … Was that it? Had they left so they could help me have an unhappy childhood? Well, it looks like it's going to happen, if I have to stay here with Uncle Corry much longer.

I don't know what happened to the pen, but I'm using the journal for the first time. I already used the video camera three times this past year. I looked at the takes again this morning and they're not bad:

1. Neighbors' cat takes a dump in our yard—zoomed in on heap.

2. Neighbors' cat runs away with the cheese from my sandwich.

3. Neighbors' cat beats up neighbors' dog. (This is the best one.)

Looking back, maybe it would have been better to film my parents.

I'm writing in this journal because:

1. Uncle Corry doesn't have a computer.

2. Uncle Corry has absolutely nothing fun to do.

3. There isn't a frigging thing to do here.

I can always go film something, but what? A movie about Uncle Corry on the couch? I don't think anybody would want to watch that. Not me, at any rate. I could shoot outside, but I don't trust this neighborhood. Before you know it, they'll have run off with your camera.

This morning I decided I'd had enough. Spent almost all of two days in my "room." (It's really more of a junk corner, with piles of old magazines all over the place. I've learned all about angling and anglers by now though.) The chocolate-sprinkle sandwiches and cheap cola are coming out my nose. Uncle Corry was once again sprawled on the couch in his favorite position. I asked him for a little money, for groceries.

"Go find a job," he said without glancing up from his *Angling and Anglers*.

Job? I'm only thirteen! I said that, but his response was that he already had three jobs when he was my age. Curious about what they were. I've never seen him do anything yet the whole time I've been here.

"I have to eat fruits and vegetables," I said.

"What for?" asked Uncle Corry.

"For the vitamins," I said.

"Why?"

Why? Hmm, I don't know exactly. I'll have to look that up—if there's a library around here at least (fat chance).

evening (after dinner) (canned navy beans in tomato sauce):
I hadn't taken two steps out the door before …

"Hey!"

A girl was sitting on the big red car parked out front. Well, not really a *girl*.

I looked around, but she must have been talking to me because she shouted, "Yeah, you over there. With the weird jacket. Come here."

Weird jacket?

I took a step in her direction.

"What are *you* doing here?"

"I uh … I'm staying with … somebody."

"What kind of somebody?"

"An uncle."

The car shook with her laughter. "That stupid old Dirkzwager at number 286?! Is that your uncle?"

I felt my face burn. It is totally no laughing matter having to admit that Uncle Corry is your uncle.

"How come?" she asked.

"Like, you know, he's my mother's brother. But—"

"No, dummy. Why are you staying there?"

Well now, was I supposed to have some sort of permit? Who did she think she was, the (back)street police?

"Like, you know," I said.

"So where are your parents?"

I took a good look at the girl. She was certainly well developed but had a funny face—round—kind of like one of those porcelain dolls. Actually her face didn't fit with the rest of her body.

"Well?"

"Well what?"

"Where are your parents?"

"Like, you know. I'm looking for a library," I said.

"How come?"

"There's something I want to find out about."

"Just ask me. I know everything. And if I don't, I make it up. Where are your parents?"

"They're … they're missing."

"What do you mean 'missing'?"

"Well, they were on a wilderness trek, in the heart of … Bulu-Bulistan. You know what I mean. And all of a sudden they disappeared."

"The heart of Bulu-Bulistan? Where's that?"

"Somewhere in Africa. Or Asia. I don't know exactly."

"I don't believe a word of it. You're making that up. I like you." She took a bill out of her pocket and waved it in the air. "It's my dad's birthday tomorrow. What should I get him?"

"Uh … well, I don't know what your dad—"

"I know. Come on."

She jumped off the car and dragged me along to a tobacco shop just down the street. "I want the best cigars there are," she announced even before we were actually inside the store.

"We don't sell tobacco products to individuals below sixteen years of age," said the man at the cash register.

"Are you nuts or something?" She slapped the bill on the counter. "Do I look like *I'm* going to smoke the stinking things myself?"

The man seemed confused for a moment. He could hardly say she looked like that, so he said, "The best cigars cost more than that, young lady. A lot more. You can get five good ones for that, but not the best, not by a long shot."

"Are they fat?"

"They certainly aren't thin."

"Are they big?"

"They're not small, that's for sure."

"Then I'll take them. Wrapped up nice."

Finally—she wasn't easily satisfied with the cigar man's wrapping skills—when we were outside again, she asked, "What's your name?"

"Rits. Maurits, really, but everybody calls me Rits."

"Never quits Rits?" She laughed. (As if I hadn't heard that one before!) "My name's Rita." She pulled me along down the sidewalk again. "That's where I live," she said, and she pointed at a house that looked just like Uncle Corry's and all the other houses on the street. "With my dad."

I didn't dare ask where her mother was. "Oh," I said.

"Come on over later tonight. Then you can meet my dad too."

"Uh … I can't."

"Why not?"

I couldn't come up quick with something good. "I have to go to the library," I said.

"It's closed tonight, dummy," she said. "Just come over tonight at eight."

It is now twelve minutes to eight.

I hope she doesn't go on and on about my parents. I don't want ANYBODY to know (except for Uncle Corry, but that couldn't be helped, he had to know) (and Steven and his parents, but there wasn't any way around that) (oh, yeah, Mrs. B too, obviously). (Well, I guess that's already a whole bunch.)

10:02 p.m.:
Rita's father is really nice. I wish I could stay *there* instead of with Uncle Corry. I'm going to bed now. I'm dead tired—tomorrow morning, the library.

Tuesday, July 5

I found some information. The woman at the library was really nice. She brought me to the medical sciences section (Dewey decimal numbers 610 to 619) and the home economics section (Dewey decimal number 640). Maybe Uncle Corry can take a look at that home economics section too sometime. They've got a lot of interesting books there, about stain removal, about decorative kitchens and stylish design for example. He could really use some tips. So, they also had a whole pile of books about vitamins and what they're needed for. My head was spinning. There are a lot more vitamins than I thought.

What I read didn't sound very good. For example (I copied this): "Vitamin C is necessary to boost immunity to infections and stress, for growth and breathing." And further on: "In the most serious cases, a deficiency of vitamin C can lead to scurvy."

Scurvy! That about gave me a heart attack. What does that look like? Do you split open? Who knows, maybe everything starts to ulcerate and fester and stink. Maybe Uncle Corry already has scurvy, because he smells really strange, like something's rotting.

So, I went to the librarian again and asked if she also had a book on scurvy, preferably with pictures.

She took me to the section with the medical books and asked what I needed it for. "A report?"

Duh! Like while I'm on vacation? Like I'm going to give reports on scurvy just for a lark. "No, for my uncle," I said. "He's probably got scurvy. And maybe I do too."

"Scurvy? Oh, really? How's that?" she wanted to know.

Not too bright, this woman—nice, but not too bright. "Because we don't eat any vitamins," I patiently explained. "We mostly have a vitamin C deficiency. Uncle Corry doesn't feel like eating any vitamins, just canned food and cola and stuff."

The librarian left. I cracked open the book, but before I was able to read a word, an old lady came over and stood next to me. "I've seen you before," she said.

I didn't feel like talking, so I said, "Could be."

"Don't you live across from me? With Cor Dirkzwager?"

"Uh, well, I do, but ..."

"I thought I'd seen you there. Yesterday. And the day before. You were probably on your way to the square, isn't that right? Taking a walk? You came back awfully quick though. It's a beautiful square, don't you think? I live at number 295, across from you."

Unbelievable! I'm being spied on by the old people's police, patrolling behind the geraniums!

"What's your name?"

"Maurits." I wanted her to go away so I could read the book, but she wasn't to be stopped. She was obviously eager for a chat. Old people are often lonely.

"That Cor doesn't seem at all like the type to take care of a child," she said. "Are things all right?"

"Sure," I said. "Fine."

"I just overheard what you said about scurvy. That doesn't sound very good."

"Well, other than that things are fine." I leaned over the book so far that my nose touched the page.

The geranium police stood there for a while. I could feel her looking at me, but now she was keeping her mouth shut, luckily.

I copied down a little about scurvy and read it aloud to Uncle Corry:

"Caused by a lack of vitamin C. The first symptoms are irritability (Uncle Corry is *very* irritable!), pain when moving (*that's* obviously why he's always lying on the couch!), bleeding—of the gums in particular—and reddish blue speckles on the skin. Later, the teeth become loose, the patient suffers from heart palpitations, and sores appear on the limbs."

Uncle Corry did not seem very impressed, but, VICTORY: he did give me a twenty. So, I'm going to go to the grocery store in a minute.

First, I'm going to have a good look in the mirror. It wouldn't surprise me at all if I had reddish blue speckles. I felt my teeth. They weren't loose yet.

Oh, yeah, at the library, I also looked at an atlas. The Democratic Republic of Congo lies deep in Africa. It's a very big country.

quarter past seven:
Went shopping. I didn't really know what to buy. Forgot to look up in those books exactly what you're supposed to eat to treat scurvy. I asked a woman who was weighing some leeks. She said she didn't know. How stupid people can be though. It seems like nobody's interested in their own health! Luckily there was another woman who did know. "You're supposed to eat fruit," she said. "Particularly citrus fruit and kiwis."

I bought a big bag of kiwis.

After that I still had to get something for dinner. I don't have a clue as to how to fix beans, or potatoes, or how to make a spaghetti sauce, which meant I bought five frozen dinners so I'd be all set for a while. Unfortunately Uncle Corry suddenly wanted to eat normal, too, so now I've only got three. (I offered him a kiwi, but he didn't want it.)

Do you know what was so cool about Rita's dad? He didn't make any trouble for me or anything. He just acted really normal to me, not like I was some kind of bothersome kid. He kept on making jokes too. I'm going over there in a little while because it's his birthday and he said I was allowed to come too—except I don't have a present.

Wednesday, July 6

It was a lot of fun being with Rita's dad. There were three of his friends there, two men and a woman—no family.

"Don't you have any family besides your dad?" I asked Rita.

I hoped she would say something about her mother, but she only said, "Sure."

My clothes stink to high heaven. Rita's dad smoked cigars the whole evening and those other folks all smoked too (cigarettes). He told stories about times past. He has done all kinds of things: sailed out on the ocean, worked in the metal industry on the scrap heap, worked in a café, and some other things I forgot. Especially the scrap heap appeals to me. You get a torch and you have to wear goggles, and then you get to burn big hunks of metal to pieces. You have to be able to tell different kinds of metal apart (seems difficult to me).

"What do you want to be?" Rita's dad asked me. (Why does everybody always want to know about that???)

"I think I'll work the scrap heap," I said. "Or else maybe I'll be a filmmaker or a writer."

Everybody had to laugh. I don't know why. They didn't laugh in an ugly way, though, the way Uncle Corry always does, so I just laughed along with them. Luckily nobody posed any ugly questions all night. Maybe I'll make a movie about Jaap (Rita's dad). At least he's done interesting things. He'll just have to not smoke so many cigars, though, because the whole take will be gray and you won't see his face.

———

Went with Rita to the pond to swim really early this morning. We were the only ones there.

The water was ice cold and then on top of that it started to rain.

"Wimp," she said when I suggested going home. So I kept on lying there in my swim trunks in the rain.

I asked if she had always lived there with her dad.

"Yeah."

"Were you born in that house?"

"No."

"Where, then?"

"Somewhere else."

"Oh."

End of conversation.

So, I asked if she felt like making a movie about her dad.

"Why?"

"I've got a camera."

"Hmm." She didn't look wildly enthusiastic. "Or we could make a movie about *your* family," she said after a while.

"My family's not all that interesting," I said.

"I think it is," she said. "Your parents disappeared. In Africa or Asia, right? That's interesting."

"But if they disappeared, we can't film them," I very cleverly pointed out.

She had nothing to say to that.

"At least *your* dad is here. We can film him," I tried again.

Rita ran into the water. "Come on in, wimp!" she shouted.

I hope I don't get sick. My teeth never chattered so hard before and my skin had a strange color when I got out of the water, reddish bluish, and I had flecks all over.

Maybe I'll have to go to the library to find out about what happens if you float around in ice-cold water too long.

evening, 5:38 p.m.:
Really weird things are happening!

This afternoon I wanted to go to the library, but just as I was going out the door, some woman appeared on the front steps.

"Are you Maurits?" she asked.

"Yes."

"I'm Tineke. Can we talk somewhere for a minute?"

I took her to my "room" because Uncle Corry was asleep on the couch.

Tineke wanted to know everything, why I was with Uncle Corry and where my parents were.

"What for?"

"I'm from the Department of Social Services," she said. "We received a report."

Report? What kind of report?

"There's a suspicion of neglect," said Tineke.

Well, that would make sense. If anybody's being neglected, it's Uncle Corry.

"Oh," I said.

"Somebody from the neighborhood called us. The person was concerned. So, we're just stopping by to see what's wrong. Maybe things aren't so bad and we won't have to do anything else."

Do? I wonder what they're going to do. Maybe put Uncle Corry in the tub and wash his clothes, comb his hair. He could also use a couple of new shirts. Maybe they can pump some vitamins into him. (They'd probably have to dope him up first, though.)

"Oh," I said.

"Is it true you're living with your uncle?"

"No. I'm staying with him. For a little while."

"Well, how long? Would you like to tell me where your parents are?"

Tineke's kind of old, twenty or thirty or something, but she's very pretty. She has long black hair and big brown eyes. She looked at me the whole time. It made me feel all funny.

"They're missing," I said. "In Africa."

Her eyes got even bigger. "How awful. Where, exactly?"

"We don't know." Not so smart of that Tineke. If you know exactly where people are, then they're not missing.

"I mean, in which country?" She talked in a soft voice and looked at me with a lot of sympathy. "Where were they last seen?"

"In the Democratic Republic of Congo."

"And how long have they been missing?"

"Oh," I said, "not very long. A week or something."

"Are they searching for them?"

"Yes. The police have set up big search parties, with airplanes and helicopters. The Democratic Republic of Congo is very big, though, and there's lots of jungle. That makes it kind of hard to search."

Tineke was quiet for a moment. (She kept looking at me.) "Don't you have any other family?" she asked.

"No."

"Something has to be done about this. I'm going to see if I can get some information on those search parties. I assume there's an embassy involved. Meanwhile, I think it would be a good idea for me to talk with your uncle for a minute." She got up.

"Uh … he's not here."

"Who's that I hear snoring, then?"

I listened. It was in fact Uncle Corry we could hear all the way over here.

"Oh. But he's very irritable. Especially if he gets woken up."

"I can handle that." Tineke went to the living room and I walked behind her. She turned around. "Just stay in your room," she said. "I want to talk with him alone for a minute."

The crack between the living-room door and the floor isn't very big in this house, which is why I couldn't hear everything. (At home that always works really well.) Luckily, though, I did hear *something*. First, they talked about eating right and child protection, then about school.

"When vacation's over, the boy will have to go to school again," I heard Tineke say. (I could hear her voice the best.)

"… kid … not …"

"But what if his parents don't come back? Then …" (Voice disappeared because a bus drove by.)

"… I'd like to hope so anyway …"

"Of course," said Tineke. "Certainly that is to be hoped. But in the worst-case scenario … find a solution."

"… hassle … situation … kid …"

"Sure. Would you happen to know more about the search?"

Things were going wrong. I had to do something. I swung the door open and dropped to the floor, groaning.

Tineke was standing next to me in a split second. "What's the matter?" she asked.

"It hurts so much. I think my stomach's splitting open."

She helped me up and looked at me with concern (big eyes). "Come on. I'm taking you to a doctor."

I just came back from there. The doctor was very nice. He talked with Tineke for a little while (no crack under the door) and then he examined me. He looked in my mouth, listened to my heart, and did a whole lot of other things besides.

"You don't have scurvy," he said. "However ..."

Here it comes, I thought. I've got something really bad.

"... you probably have ..."

Likely something much worse than scurvy.

"... problems due to stress. Isn't that so?"

"Well, a little, sometimes," I said.

"You can get quite a stomachache from that. I think it would be a good idea to have a talk with somebody."

"I'm already doing that. I talk with Tineke. Do I need lots of medicine?"

"No," said the doctor. "Medicine won't be necessary. But you do have to promise that you'll talk about your problems—with Tineke or with somebody else. If there isn't anybody, come see me."

"Okay," I said.

Tineke brought me home again. She gave me a little card with her name and phone number on it. "I'm going to see what I can do for you," she said. "If anything comes up, you can always call me. I'll be by again soon."

Uncle Corry was furious. He was sitting on the couch (sitting up!), cursing and carrying on. What was that broad doing here and how did she happen to come over here and where did she get the stinking nerve to mess around in his business? He didn't even ask how things had gone at the doctor's or whether I maybe had a deadly disease. So, I quickly went to my "room" and that's why I'm sitting here now.

In a little while, I'll sneak out and go see Rita. Maybe I'll be allowed to stay for dinner. If only I could stay there *all the time*.

Seeing how much I wrote today, I guess I'll be a writer. There's a lot more to write about than to film!

Thursday, July 7

And it doesn't ever stop. Last night when Rita stepped out to go to the bathroom, Jaap (Rita's dad) all of a sudden said, "Listen, Rits, I'd like to ask you something. Are you going with Rita to her aunt's funeral tomorrow?"

Funeral? I didn't even know she *had* an aunt, never mind that her aunt had died.

"I feel that Rita should go. It's her family, after all, but she doesn't want to go alone."

Then why wasn't he going? If it was *her* aunt, isn't it his family too? "Oh," I said.

Jaap was quiet for a moment. "I can't go," he finally said, as if he could read my mind. "It's at twelve thirty," he added. "You don't have to wear anything special—just the way you are is fine. I'll give you two money for a cab there and back."

A cab! I've never been in a cab.

"Okay," I said.

Slept really badly last night. I've never gone to a funeral before—not one I can remember, at least. My last grandmother died when I was four. I don't remember anything about it anymore. How do they do a funeral? Are you supposed to look into the coffin? And what are you supposed to say to all those people? What if you have a laughing fit or have to puke?

evening:
Again, all kinds of things going on!

The cab was great. Rita and I sat together in the back seat and we flew through the streets at a crazy speed. You hardly felt the engine. It was as if we were floating (but super fast). I want a car like that someday (although I forgot to look at the model).

"Is it hard to become a cab driver?" I asked the driver.

"No, not at all," he said. "You have to be able to steer a little bit, and knowing your way around helps."

I think I can do that, although I'm not sure I'd be good at remembering my way around.

"So, you want to be a cab driver?" the driver asked. The car suddenly shot forward and veered around a corner. He laughed. "Gotta take advantage of a yellow light."

Rita had been un-Rita-likely quiet until then, but that was all over now. "Act like a normal person, man," she shouted at the driver. "You want to get us killed or something?"

The driver looked around and grinned at me. "Well? You want to be a cab driver?"

"Uh ... yeah, I think so," I said when I was sitting up straight again.

"The street's *over there!*" Rita cried, pointing at the wind-shield. "Watch where you're going."

"Being a cab driver is really a man's job," said the driver. He was watching where he was going again, luckily. "The ladies don't have the nerves for it." He laughed loudly.

"The ladies aren't mentally deficient enough for it," said Rita. After that she said no more and kept staring out the window.

U. C.'s calling me.

—

Uncle Corry said that "she" had called (Tineke). She had said nothing was known about a Dutch couple that had disappeared. He asked what that meant.

"Like, you know," I said.

"*Jesus*. You told her that your parents went missing in the Congo? Why on earth did you do that?"

"The Democratic Republic of Congo," I said. "That's something entirely different." Uncle Corry's not one of the brightest people around either. Congo's an entirely different country! It's next to the Democratic Republic of Congo, but it's a lot smaller.

"Why? Why did you tell her that?"

"Like, you know," I said. "It's nobody's business. You said so yourself yesterday. 'What business is it of hers?' you said."

Uncle Corry grumbled some more, but he couldn't say I was wrong, obviously. "We have to make sure that girl stays away from here," he said. "She said she'd stop by later."

"When?"

"She didn't say."

"So, we just don't open the door when the doorbell rings," I said. I felt a little weird because all of a sudden Uncle Corry and I were ganging up together, and we were doing that even though I think Tineke's nice and he's not! I don't feel like having any more problems though. I already have enough.

"I bought some apples," said Uncle Corry. "They're in the kitchen. Eat them whenever you want. And there's orange juice."

Why is he suddenly being so nice? I don't get it. But it does come in handy. If this keeps up, maybe I can ask him for a computer. My hand is getting cramped from all this writing.

Friday, July 8

6:32 a.m., still in bed:
I couldn't write anymore yesterday. The longer I thought about my cramped-up hand, the more cramped it got. In the end it got so cramped that I could hardly move it. I wasn't even writing anymore! I wasn't doing anything!

So, now I'm going to try to write about everything that happened at the funeral yesterday in a short summary, or else my hand will cramp up in no time, *again*. Yesterday, I had all these thoughts about my hand having to be amputated. That doesn't seem like a whole lot of fun. You can't do a lot of things then. For example, how do you wash dishes with one hand? I suppose you could buy yourself a dishwasher. Maybe you'd even get one for free from the hospital. Now that might be cool.

— We got to the funeral.

— We watched the cab scream down the driveway and around the corner (tires squealing, nice sound).

— There were lots of people at the funeral.

— It wasn't a burial. It was a cremation.

— There was no place to sit in the waiting area.

— I didn't know anybody.

— Rita knew some people. She said hi to some of them, but didn't really talk with anybody (not much with me either).

— We went into the chapel.

— There was a coffin in it.

— We didn't have to look into it.

— The coffin was closed.

— Three people said something about the aunt into the microphone.

— The aunt was a very nice woman. Her name was Sara. She did a lot for people. She did a lot and then some. She had a great sense of humor when she was still alive.

— We left the chapel.

— In another room there were sandwiches.

— It was really boring there.

Now, here it comes. I can't write a summary of this. Okay, I'll try.

Rita and I were standing in a corner. We decided to play "who could eat the most sandwiches." (Actually Rita decided. I was just glad that she was starting to talk again.) The trouble was that the sandwiches were lying on these high, round tables, and we didn't have a table so we didn't have any sandwiches either. There were lots of people standing around all the tables. We had to figure out how to get those sandwiches off the tables. Rita did it easily. She just went over, squeezed her way into a group of people, and returned in a flash with three sandwiches.

"How many sandwiches do you think you're allowed?" I asked her.

"What difference does that make?" she responded.

"Can I have one of yours?"

"Get your own sandwiches."

Oh, right, *that's* when we decided to see who could eat the most sandwiches. Okay, doesn't really matter. I went over to a table and hung around a little, looking for an opening.

"I think it's a shame," I heard a woman with short curly hair say.

"Isn't it though!" said another woman, who also had short curly hair. "And he doesn't even come with her. Just doesn't have much backbone, that's all."

"To think he let her come here all by herself," said a third woman, who also had short curly hair. I couldn't see her face, but she sounded teed off. "You just don't do something like that."

"She's just a child."

"I can understand he didn't dare to come," said the first woman. "It's nothing to sneeze at, any of it. And on top of that, the *entire family's* here."

"The *entire family*," repeated the third woman with short curly hair.

(There was a woman with short straight hair, too, but she didn't say anything.)

"She really ought to know sometime," said the first woman.

"Of course he never told her a thing. So, she doesn't know anything, about any of it."

"He simply keeps her away from her own family. That's the worst part of it, I think. He's obviously afraid she'll find out."

"It's a miracle she was allowed to come," said the first woman. "Although she *has* been keeping to herself all this time. Well, I guess she's with some boy or other."

"Oh? Where is she?"

Here it comes.

"There." The woman pointed at our corner. They were talking about Rita! (And that made me the "some boy or other." I mean, really!)

"He simply doesn't dare show his face," said the second woman. "That figures."

"But it really is a shame, altogether," said the first woman. "Mother dead and on top of that hardly any contact with her family."

"When you think about what he did …," said the third woman.

"Somebody like that you'd just as soon—"

"It makes me wonder: What kind of a world are we living in?"

All the women shook their heads (even the one with the short straight hair).

"It's all *his* fault," said the first woman.

All the women nodded.

(This conversation was just about the way I've written it down here, although I don't remember who said what exactly anymore. All those women looked alike. And because I had to make sure they didn't see me, I couldn't get *too* close. So, I missed a remark now and then.)

I stole back (without sandwiches) to Rita. "I have to go to the bathroom," I said. It wasn't true, but I needed time to think. So, Rita's mother was dead! Boy, was I ever glad I hadn't asked about her.

The rest of the conversation went by me. There was obviously something going on that Rita doesn't know about and/or isn't supposed to know about. It sounded really bad. It's all *his* fault, they said. What is *whose* fault? Who's the "he"? Jaap? But what did he do that's so bad?

I didn't know what to do. Tell Rita what I'd heard?

"Who are those people?" I asked when I came back from the bathroom. I pointed at the table of women.

"The score is 3–0, doofus. Where are your sandwiches?"

Why didn't that girl ever answer normally?! I'd had it. "Okay, I'll just go over there and ask," I said, and I made motions to go to the table. (Not that I would have done it, obviously. I know better than that. It worked though.)

"No!" Rita pulled me back with a hard tug on my T-shirt. "Stay here."

"Who are those women?"

She let go of me. "Friends of my aunt's. Why are you asking?"

"They were gossiping about ... all kinds of stuff."

"Oh, yeah? What about, then? What did you hear?"

"Like, you know."

"Well, then don't tell me. Come on, we're going." Rita shoved me in the direction of the door. All of a sudden, though, a man stopped us.

"Hello there, Marguerite," said the man.

Marguerite?

"Hi," said Rita.

"How are you? How's Jaap?"

"Fine."

"Too bad we hardly ever get to see you anymore."

"We've been busy."

"We'd like it if you came by sometime. You're welcome to bring your boyfriend." The man nodded in my direction.

"That's not my boyfriend."

"Oh, well, all right, but that's no reason for you not to bring him along, is it?"

"I'll see."

We kept on walking, headed into the foyer. Rita had a cab

called, and ten minutes later we were on our way home (with a female cab driver!). (All went well.) Again, Rita just stared out the window and didn't say a word.

What the hey is going on? Well, I better not get involved. My life's complicated enough already.

later (still in bed):
The sun's out. I don't feel like getting up. SOMETHING HAS TO HAPPEN! Things can't go on like this. But I don't know *what* should happen. So, I'll just stay in bed. Maybe a miracle will happen—something like an angel appearing at the foot of my bed, saying, "Everything's all right again. You can go home." But it's broad daylight. Angels don't appear in broad daylight and certainly not to me. All night I tossed and turned, and guess what? Nothing. No angel, not a one! On top of that, I don't believe in angels, so I'm sure they don't feel like appearing to me. I'm sure there's no use in waiting around, hoping one will. I kept thinking of Rita's aunt Sara in her coffin. I knew what she looked like only after she was dead (photo near coffin) (of when she was still alive). It's strange getting to know somebody only after he or she is already dead. And now she's nothing but a pile of ashes. It can happen that fast. I'm sure she had a scary disease.

Why doesn't my dad come pick me up? I don't even know where he is. He doesn't know where I am either. He might well be dead. Why is Uncle Corry my uncle? Why don't I have a normal uncle, like other kids do? When other kids' parents are gone, *they* have at least a hundred nice family members they can go stay with, but I have nobody but Uncle Corry.

So, something has to be done—but what? The possibilities:

— I steal money and take the train home. I stay there and live by myself. I go out and break into places to get money until I'm old enough to work.

— I go look for my dad. I do know roughly where he is, in which part of the world, I mean. I'll just start a search.

— I go ask if I can live with Jaap and Rita for a little while.

— I stay here and wait.

The third possibility appeals to me the most, but I don't really dare. They'll want to know what's going on, of course. Besides, maybe I wouldn't even be allowed to.

I've got an idea. I'll wait another week. If nothing has happened by then, I'll go ask if I can live with Jaap. If I'm not allowed to, I'll steal money and become a burglar. Then I can go live at home and maybe also look for my dad.

I already feel a little better. I'll get up in a minute.

I think Rita's pretty nice, but she never talks about anything. Weird. Doesn't she have any girlfriends or anything? She never says anything about other kids. I'm going to question her good sometime soon, but first, a quick trip to the library.

later:

I was eating breakfast (four slices of white bread with chocolate sprinkles) when the doorbell rang. Uncle Corry and I looked at each other. Neither of us did anything. I didn't dare chew anymore. The doorbell rang again, and again. It cost a whole lot of effort not to get up and answer the door. I was sure it was Tineke, but maybe it was Rita or my dad, who was coming to pick me up. I felt rotten about it. We can't just never answer the door again.

Finally I couldn't take it anymore and ran to the front door, but whoever had rung the doorbell was gone.

"We weren't going to answer the door," said Uncle Corry when I came back into the living room.

"Maybe it was somebody else," I said.

"Then again, maybe it wasn't," said Uncle Corry.

"I'll go see Tineke this afternoon," I said. "I'll tell her she doesn't have to come over anymore, that my parents are back, that everything's fine again." I felt around in the pocket of my pants. I still had her card. "Then we can go ahead and answer the door again."

"On the other hand, I think it's fine the way it is," said Uncle Corry. "Nice and quiet."

"How much longer am I supposed to stay here?"

"You're welcome to leave."

I understand very well why my mom never wanted to see Uncle Corry. Whenever I asked anything about him when I was little—I hadn't ever seen him yet even—she always said he was a drip. Now I think I know what that word means.

"You don't think much of staying here, do you?"

I didn't feel like saying that that was in fact the truth, but I didn't feel like lying either. So I didn't say anything.

"Oh, but then you're used to living better, what with your expensive house and your expensive clothes."

This conversation was going entirely in the wrong direction. I wasn't in the mood to talk with him about things like that.

"Your mother had it all figured out," he went on, "with that artsy type." He chuckled. "At least she thought she did."

"Artsy type?"

"Your father. She found them interesting, those artsy types that paint paintings and whatnot. But now you see what comes of all that."

"What does come of all that?"

"Misery. Believe me, your mother's no better than me."

"Than I," I say.

"Huh?"

"Than I. You're saying it wrong. You said 'better than me.' It's 'better than I.'" It always totally annoys me when my parents correct me, but it was handy having a trick weapon to wield. It had little effect though. Uncle Corry looked like a goldfish being taught math. "Never mind. Tell me something about my mother. What was she like when she was young?" Stupid, maybe, asking that out of the blue. Cozying up to Uncle Corry was the last thing I felt like doing, but I wanted to talk about my parents with somebody who knew them. Unfortunately I had nobody but him for that.

"We used to fight all the time," he said.

"About what?"

"Don't recall." He picked up his *Angling and Anglers* from the table.

"Tell me something about your parents—my grandpa and grandma." Now that we were finally having a conversation, or something resembling one, I wasn't planning to give up just like that.

"What?" He didn't look up from his *Angling and Anglers*.

"What were they like? Were they nice? What kind of life did they have?"

"They were born. They lived. They died."

I should have known. Trying to have a normal conversation with Uncle Corry is a waste of time. I got up and went to my cubbyhole. So now I'm sitting here (again!) writing. If I were to be honest: all this writing is driving me crazy. I'd like to do something else for a change, but I keep having the funny feeling that I have to write down everything that's going on because it's important, so I'll remember it later—although it's easier to imagine that I'd rather forget it all.

I'm going over to Rita's—maybe she'll think of something fun to do—or to the library first.

later:
Tonight I'm going to hear a rock band!! Rita asked me if I'd go.

"Is your dad letting you go?"

"Of course."

The band's called The Geeks. They're playing in the music hall at The Cornerstone, a café nearby. It's a hard rock band that uses Dutch lyrics, Rita said. I've never been to a live performance before.

Haven't gone to see Tineke yet.

Just called Tineke at work. She wasn't there. She won't be back until Monday, they said. I told Uncle Corry that we could go ahead and answer the door until Monday because Tineke's off work. Go figure, nobody will ring the doorbell all weekend.

Stopped in at the library to look up something about sagging brain. I couldn't find anything, and yet I have the feeling my brains are sagging. Yesterday and today I had a funny feeling in my head all the time, not really pain, but ... I don't know how to describe it—like something was pushing on my brain, pushing it down, causing it to sag. The encyclopedia did have all kinds of information about brain tumors. Maybe this is the beginning of one, or else I've got a new disease that's still unknown. If this keeps up, maybe I'll have to write them sometime, the encyclopedia people. Maybe they just forgot about the subject. It's possible, because there are a huge number of diseases. I think it must be hard to remember them all.

I'm going over to Jaap and Rita's for supper in a minute. I keep hoping they'll say, "Just come and stay, we've got a spare bed," but they keep not saying it.

Saturday, July 9

This morning I woke up with a really weird ringing in my ears, like there was a kettle whistling in my head. Could it have something to do with the sagging brain thing? It's already a little better now.

The Geeks were awesome—their music, anyway. I couldn't understand the lyrics. Rita said it was Dutch, but it might as well have been Japanese or even Democratic Republic of Congoese. Rita had seen The Geeks a few times before. A girlfriend's brother is in the band, she said. (Aha, so she *does* have girlfriends.) The place was really crowded. As far as I could tell, we were the youngest people there. I proposed we order some beers so we wouldn't stand out, but Rita thought I shouldn't act so dumb. "Beer's disgusting," she said and got two colas. Luckily nobody looked at us funny—we must look older than we are, even without beer.

The Geeks looked awesome. They were all wearing bright blue suits and white ties and had ski hats and heavy black-rimmed glasses on. When they started playing, we couldn't talk anymore. Now and then I saw Rita looking at me while her mouth moved, but what she was saying I couldn't hear. I moved my mouth a little, too. The music, though!! Never knew guitars could sound like *that*. It felt like my brains were being sliced down the middle. And those drums—the sound pounded straight through my body. All my innards were bouncing up and down. Super! I totally felt alive—pie in the sky, like I *was* the music or something.

"I'm going to be a rock musician too," I said to Rita during the break.

"Oh yeah? You play an instrument?"

"Uh … I'm going to buy a drum set," I said.

"And where are you going to get the thousand euros?"

Sometimes she's a real downer, that girl. Why does she have to come up with problems the minute I think of something cool? But she was right, I don't have a penny to my name. Rita—or, rather, Jaap—paid for my ticket and the cola too. Things can't go on like this. I have to find a way to get some money. I'm going to think about that. Finish this story first, though, since a lot more things happened.

It was already midnight by the time The Geeks stopped playing. I was pretty tired, but Rita didn't want to go home yet.

"Does your dad let you stay out this late?" I asked.

"My dad's not home," she said. "How about you? Does your uncle want you to go to bed?"

"Like it matters to him."

"Admit it," she went on. "That stupid old Corry Dirkzwager won't let you stay out too late."

"Oh, give me a break," I snapped. "He doesn't give a rat's ass how late I come home. Nobody does. If I'm dead, nobody'd care." I ran to the bathroom and locked the door. I had never yelled at Rita before. I'm sure it took her by surprise. I waited for her to come after me.

After about five minutes, somebody started pounding on the door. "Open up, dude. You've been in there an hour already. I have to go too." I unlocked the door and walked out. A guy with blue spiked hair gave me an angry look.

I went back into the music hall. There was Rita, sitting at the bar, next to a Geek. They were deep in conversation. The Geek wasn't wearing glasses anymore and he'd also taken off his hat. I went over to them. Rita didn't see me, or acted as if she didn't.

She just kept on talking to that stupid Geek, and by the look on her face he was saying all kinds of totally interesting things.

Actually that was true. They were talking about music. I tried to follow the conversation. He was talking about how much money they got for gigs (I didn't understand how much, but I could tell from Rita's face that it was a lot), and about how successful they were. They were recording a CD, said the Geek, because there were always lots of people at their gigs who wanted to buy a CD.

I wish *I* played with The Geeks. Then I'd be earning loads of money, with gigs and CD sales, and be able to buy cola for my friends. Now the Geek was doing that. He ordered cola for Rita and beer for himself and nothing for me.

I tugged at Rita's shirt. "I'm going to take off," I said.

"Huh? Oh, you were still here?"

That was the last straw. Without saying good-bye, I turned around and walked out, through the café, and down the street. Stupid twit. As soon as she had somebody else to talk to she didn't take notice of me anymore. Of course she didn't have any girlfriends or boyfriends. Who'd want to be friends with a dip like that? Not me. I'd had enough!

I stopped short. I had simply left her there with a strange Geek. Soon she'd have to walk home all by herself. It was only three blocks, but still … in the middle of the night … in a neighborhood full of creeps. What should I do? I was angry. Keep walking. I was worried. Go back. Angry. Keep walking. Worried. Go back. Keep walking. Go back. I don't know how long I stood there, but suddenly I heard a voice. "Hey there, dummy!"

Rita. She ran over to me. "What are you standing there for?"

"I don't feel like sleeping," I said.

"Come with me. We can stay up as long as we want. My dad's not around anyway."

"Where is he?" I asked as we walked along together.

"At my grandma's in Zeeland."

"How come you didn't go?"

"Didn't feel like it. I'm old enough to stay at home alone."

"But what if something happens?"

"Like what?"

"Well, a fire or something, or a burglar."

"Then I'll call the fire department or the police, or I'll go to the neighbor lady. She used to baby-sit all the time when my dad had to go away. You know who I'm talking about. She was there at my dad's birthday party."

"Aren't you scared when you're home alone?"

"What should I be scared of?"

She was probably right. I think burglars and characters like that would rather choose a house *without* Rita. I was glad I hadn't said that I'd been worried about her. She would have laughed right in my face.

"You want to tell spooky stories?" Rita was lying on her back on the living-room floor. I was sitting up, leaning against the couch.

I don't know why I suddenly said it, why I suddenly dared to. Maybe it was because I had been so worked up before. Maybe it was because it was the middle of the night and I was so tired that I couldn't think straight anymore. Suddenly I asked, "Do you miss her?"

It was quiet for a moment. "Who?" she asked.

"Your mother."

"What do you know about my mother?"

"Nothing," I said. "I know she isn't around." I didn't dare say I knew she was dead.

"It's okay." Again silence.

"What's okay?"

"It's okay that I miss her." She rolled over on her stomach. "Spooky story?"

"No," I said. "I'm wasted. I have to get some sleep."

"You don't dare. You're scared of spooky stories."

"I'm tired." I got up.

"There once was a boy who lived with his uncle. What he didn't know was, his uncle was a werewolf. All month long nothing unusual happened. His uncle would quietly lie on the couch and read a magazine. But at midnight on the full moon, he changed into a horrible hairy monster with sharp teeth that dripped blood. He'd already eaten the boy's parents."

"I'm going."

"First the father, then the mother. He had torn them to pieces and gobbled them up, and what he couldn't finish, he put in the freezer for later. That way he wouldn't need to go shopping for the rest of the month. It was—"

"I'm really going home," I said.

"One night the boy went to his uncle's house. It was a full moon, just like now."

"Bye." I walked down the hallway and opened the front door.

"I'll come by tomorrow afternoon," I heard her shout, "to see if there are any pieces of you left in the freezer."

I slammed the door.

—

The street was empty and quiet. I looked up. The sky was cloudy, so it was hard to tell if there really was a full moon, but I thought it was. I felt myself get uneasy—that girl and her stupid story. I ran the last stretch to the front door and quickly stuck the key in the lock. Strange, there was a light burning in the hallway.

I carefully opened the door and peered inside—nobody. I stepped into the hallway, let the door softly fall shut in the lock, and stole past the living room. Did I hear something? I stood still and pricked up my ears—nothing. A little light shone through the crack under the living-room door though. Somebody was there! And that somebody was staying very quiet. My heartbeat throbbed through my head as I snuck farther.

The door flew open. A yell—there stood Uncle Corry, a wild look in his big bloodshot eyes. His hair was stuck to his forehead. In his fist, he was holding an enormous baseball bat that he raised toward me. I screamed. He screamed. I couldn't move, stood nailed to the ground as if I'd been frozen fast. We stared at each other. Uncle Corry's eyes were opened wide.

"Christamighty," he said. He lowered the baseball bat. "Is that you? Jesus."

"Y-yeah." There was a strange quiver in my voice.

"I thought it was an intruder," he said. "Are you out of your mind? What are you doing up so late? And why are you sneaking around the house like a thief?"

"I was trying to be quiet. I thought you were already asleep."

"I thought *you* had gone to bed a long time ago."

"I went to see The Geeks with Rita."

"The what? Geez, that sobered me up in a hurry." Uncle Corry went into the living room. I walked in behind him.

"So where did you go?" I asked.

"You know, to the café down the street, The WunderBar. I always throw a beer in the tank there on Fridays. With my buddies. At The WunderBar."

If you ask me, he'd hoisted more than one. If you ask me, the tank was good and full.

Uncle Corry went to the kitchen and returned with two bottles of beer.

"Gotta catch my breath," he said. He pressed one of the bottles into my hand. "Here, so you can catch your breath too."

"Beer's disgusting," I said and took a sip. Eeyuk! I swallowed and was determined that that sip would also be my last one, forever.

Uncle Corry quickly tossed down the whole bottle. (I mean its contents.) He lay down on the couch.

I got an awesome idea. "Here, have this one too." I gave him my bottle of beer, which he eagerly grabbed. "No more for me, thanks."

Crazy people and drunks always tell the truth, isn't that right? At least that's what my dad says. Since both descriptions now applied to Uncle Corry, I had a fine opportunity to question him about my mom.

I'll write the rest down later. I don't feel like it anymore. My hand's starting to feel funny again as it is.

± 7:00 p.m.:
The sky's about to fall. I just don't know

Monday, July 11

Last night I lay there thinking: I've been in existence for thirteen years already (and in four months and seventeen days, a whole fourteen years!). That's a pretty long time, although when I try to think back over the entire time I existed, I can't really even remember all that much of it. Nothing really earth-shattering or weird or ugly ever happened. Probably all the earth-shattering and weird and ugly things got saved up until now. Now they're suddenly coming all at the same time. Couldn't it be distributed a little better? I don't think it's nice at all (except for one thing that *is* nice, but I'll get to that). It just goes on and there seems to be no end to it. I'm going to try to write everything down, but then in brief, because again so much has happened the past few days that it already makes me tired just thinking about how much work it'll be to write it down. (I have to watch out for my hand too.)

Saturday afternoon I didn't feel like sitting at home anymore. I went downtown (a long, long way to walk, no money for the bus)—not to do anything special, just to hang around a little and look in the store windows. Meanwhile, I was thinking of ways to get some money.
— Look for a job. But where and what? I don't think the world's holding its breath, waiting for thirteen-year-old boys. I'm going to ask Uncle Corry what he did when he was my age. Didn't he say he had three jobs by that time? No, better yet, I'll ask Jaap. He's got much better ideas for sure.
— Steal. But I don't know if I can do that—maybe I could if I

stole from a really mean person because then it's not pathetic. But how do you know if somebody's really mean? Of course I could try to steal money from Uncle Corry, but I don't think that'll work.

— Beg. I don't know if I dare do that. You're pretty much standing there like a fool if you do that.

— Play music and go around with a hat. This is the best way, but the problem is I can't buy an instrument because I don't have any money. Besides, I can't play one (although that doesn't matter because I don't have an instrument anyway). Maybe I can borrow The Geeks' drum set and get lessons at the same time. But lessons cost money too.

Crap. You need a whole lot of money to be able to earn money.

After a couple of hours, I walked back to Uncle Corry's house. I remembered I still had to find a way to wangle some money out of him to buy groceries. Otherwise, we wouldn't have anything to eat all weekend besides apples and kiwis.

"That girl was here," said Uncle Corry.

I was startled. "Tineke?"

"No, that girlfriend of yours from down the street."

"Oh."

"She said you two had planned something."

"Huh?" I couldn't remember anything about that.

"She waited for you in your room for quite a while."

Wait a minute. Oh yeah, she said something Friday night. When I was leaving, she said she would come by the next day to see if there were any pieces of me left in the freezer. That was true too, but I'd thought it was one of those typical Rita jokes.

"Suddenly I heard her stomping down the hall and outside. She slammed the door. Strange chick."

A silence fell. I got a nasty feeling. Why? Something was up, but what? A chill ran through my bones, slowly, from my head to my toes—colder and icier all the time. Everything in me started to freeze up.

My body felt as heavy as a rhinoceros. I don't know how, but somehow or other I managed to get it to move anyway. Inch by inch I shuffled in the direction of my cubbyhole—like in a dream. The door was slightly open. No, not like in a dream, it was like I was acting in a horror movie and watching it at the same time. The door came closer in slow motion, close-up of the latch. I pushed the door open a little more and prepared myself for the most horrible sight.

There it lay, open and exposed on my bed. If a bleeding, cut-open corpse had lain there, I couldn't have had a worse scare. It was true. The worst that could have happened had happened. Rita had read my journal.

If the movie had been in slow motion before, it now went into fast-forward. Like somebody obsessed, I read everything I'd written in the hopes of finding that there wasn't anything bad in it—nothing insulting, nothing I'd have to be ashamed of.

Of course it was absolutely full of those kinds of things.

I had clamped my right index finger between the pages to which my journal had been opened when I found it (even in a crisis I'm still relatively together), so I could remember to where she had read—not to the end, at any rate.

It wasn't necessary for me to do that, though, the finger thing, I mean—because I already knew.

Her aunt's funeral. The cab. The sandwich contest. Just one last page lay on my finger. I turned it with a shaky hand (which was strange because I knew exactly what was coming, even though I hoped a miracle had happened so that suddenly something totally different would be described there).

The Conversation at the Sandwich Table.

How asinine of me! Why do I insist on writing everything so exactly? I could just as easily have written: some women were standing near the sandwich table. They were having a conversation. Period.

Why didn't I hide my journal? It just never occurred to me that Rita would sit here all by herself. I'm not afraid of Uncle Corry. He never reads anything that's not about angling and anglers. He's not at all interested in me anyway, so why would he go and read my journal? He doesn't even know I write in it.

What now what now what now?

I had to do something. I must have lain on my bed for an hour. Then I thought: I'm going to write about everything. Maybe then my mind will calm down again. But just when I had started, Uncle Corry called me. I had a phone call. I took the receiver from him.

"Hi there, Rits." Jaap.

"Howdy."

"Do you know where Rita is? There was a message saying she had gone over to your house and would be back home around six."

I looked at the clock. It was ten past seven.

"Your uncle said she was over at your place but that she left again."

"Yes," I said. "No. I don't know where she is."

If a guilty feeling could be expressed in miles, then mine was about as big as the Democratic Republic of Congo.

"So, what did she say?"

"Nothing. I mean, I didn't see her."

"How do you mean? She was over at your place, wasn't she?"

"I wasn't home."

There was a silence that seemed to last half an hour.

"If you see her, tell her that she should come home right away."

"I'll do that." To heck with the Democratic Republic of Congo—as big as all of Africa.

"Thanks. Bye, Rits."

"Bye."

My mind was cranking at full speed. The only good thing about the whole situation was that I was no longer bothered by sagging brain. From shock, it had flopped back to its normal spot.

Where could she be? What was I supposed to do? It was all my fault. I *had* to do something.

"So, the kid's missing," said Uncle Corry, obviously wanting to say something sensible at least.

"Yeah. I have to find her." I said it more to myself than to him.

"She'll turn up again on her own. Your mother used to go missing at the drop of a hat."

I threw him the most poisonous, deadliest look I had in me. Why did he have to suddenly start in about my mom of his own accord *now*? (By the way, this makes me think of Friday night when I had gotten him to talk with a couple of extra beers. I still have to write that down.) But instead of dropping dead, the way he really should have, he calmly lowered himself down on the couch and picked up his *Angling and Anglers.*

I must have roamed through the neighborhood for at least three hours. Searching is a shitty activity. At every corner you think: There! That's where she'll be, around the corner, and everything will be okay again—but no. She wasn't around any corner—not behind any tree, not under any car, not in any portico. I started to doubt that I would ever see her again alive.

It was already getting dark when I walked past her house. It occurred to me that she might have gone back home long ago. Who knows? Maybe she was calmly lying in her bed while I was running around like a half-wit looking for her. I could ring the doorbell, but what if she wasn't there? What was I supposed to say to Jaap then? I decided I'd go home first. Maybe Jaap or Rita had called in the meantime to say that everything was okay.

Jaap had in fact called, but everything was not okay. Uncle Corry said that Rita still wasn't home. Jaap had asked if I'd stop by.

"What time did he call?" I asked.

"Just now. Ten minutes ago."

Now I understand exactly what they mean when they talk about having "lead in your shoes." I dragged pounds of it along as I made my way over the short distance from Uncle Corry's house to Rita's house. My head was empty. I didn't know what I was supposed to think anymore, never mind what I was supposed to say to Jaap. Well then, the truth? But what *was* the truth? I didn't understand it myself. I only knew that something had happened, something that was very bad, and that that "something" was my fault.

I rang the doorbell. The door opened.

"Easy now," said Jaap. He threw his arm around me and brought me over to the couch in the living room. "You don't need to cry. She's already been found. I know where she is."

I looked at him. I tried to say something (I don't remember what), but only a strange squeak came out of my throat. Jaap walked off and returned with a big glass of water. "Here, drink some of this," he said.

In silence we sat beside each other on the couch. I took little sips of water. The only sound in the room was the ticking of the clock—and my swallowing. I tried to do it as quietly as possible, but each time it sounded like a thunderclap was rolling through the room.

"Something happened," said Jaap when I had emptied the glass. "I have an idea what it is, but I want to know for sure."

"So, what is it?" Luckily normal sounds were coming out of my throat again.

"I was hoping you could tell me that."

"Didn't Rita say anything?"

"No. She's with her aunt. That's the person who called me."

"Aunt? But she's dead." I felt really stupid as I was saying that—as if he didn't know—but it just flopped out.

"She has other aunts."

"Could I have some more water?" I wasn't thirsty, but I wanted to stretch the time.

Jaap didn't fall for it. "In a minute," he said. "First just tell me everything you know."

My throat started to close up.

"Whatever it is, I promise I won't get angry," he said. "Honest, I won't get angry."

There was no escaping it. I had to tell. "She read my journal," I said.

Jaap looked somewhat relieved. (What on earth for?!) "Oh, really? What kind of journal?"

"A kind ... a journal you write things in and stuff."

"You mean a diary?"

I nodded as a feeling of shame shot through me like a tongue of fire—so fiercely, it just plain hurt: a boy with a diary. What must Jaap have thought? But right after that I was ashamed of the fact that I was ashamed, as if that mattered now. There were more important things—far more important things.

"And what was in there? Had you written something unkind about her?"

"Well ... not really. It was more ..."

"Just say it. I won't get angry. Honest."

"It was about the funeral ... I mean cremation."

Jaap appeared to be startled. "What about it?"

"I overheard a conversation among some women."

Jaap was now staring straight ahead. "Go on," he said.

"Well, like, they were talking about Rita and that she was there all by herself and that her mom was dead."

"And then?"

I looked at the floor. "They were talking about a 'he' who must have done something. That's all I know."

"What did they say exactly? Try to remember. I want to know."

Jaap's voice sounded sharp. When I glanced up and saw his eyes, I shrank back. His gaze ran right through me. I was scared for a minute. I had thought of it once but didn't dare to think it because it was too awful to think. Could Jaap have murdered

Rita's mom? I couldn't have imagined that earlier, but now I almost could, seeing the way he looked. There I was, alone in a house with a man who was maybe a murderer! It was better if I made something up, something that would satisfy him. My mind was working full speed, but it was totally blank, like there was nothing in it and never had been.

Jaap got up. "Come on. We'll go get your diary."

"I remember!"

He sat down.

"They were talking about a 'he.' They said that he had done something very bad and that Rita didn't know that and that it was all very bad and that he didn't dare come to the funeral because the whole family was there and that it was all *his* fault. The *he's* fault, that is."

Jaap cursed a good number of times (a lot more than you'd expect of somebody who wasn't getting angry), and with each curse I felt myself grow smaller and smaller. I wasn't even scared anymore. I only wished I could disappear, become invisible—be gone from here, from the whole rotten situation, be home, with my parents, in my own bed—but I wasn't at home and wasn't invisible either.

Jaap sat down beside me again. He heaved the deepest sigh I ever heard. "I'll tell you," he said. "Maybe you can help."

Help. Me? You don't ask an elephant to help tidy up the china shop. How would *I* be able to help? Sure, from the frying pan into the fire, I was good at that. For the rest, though, I couldn't imagine how anybody would ever be able to tolerate the help, the presence, or even just the *existence* of Maurits Hofmeijer.

—

It's quarter to three. I have to quit. I'll write more tonight. I've got an appointment with Tineke in a minute. I hope not so much will happen for a little while, because I'm still running behind. All of this was just Saturday. After that, there's still Sunday and then today, that's Monday.

P.S. I found a great way to get hold of some money. That's the nice thing I brought up earlier.

evening (still Monday):
Jaap gave me the address of the aunt and uncle. Rita had spent the night there and he thought it would be a good idea for me to stop by and talk with her. So, I went over there Sunday morning. To be honest, I didn't really feel like it. All the hassle—that it would be *me* of all people who had to end up in a situation like that again. I have nothing to do with it, but I'm left holding everybody's bags. How can *I* help it that she read my diary and that this caused *their* royal mess to come to light?

Rita's aunt opened the door. "You're Rits," she said. "Jaap called ahead to say you were coming. Come in."

She didn't mention what *her* name was. What was I supposed to call her, "Rita's aunt"?

Sitting in the living room was a man who looked familiar to me.

"Hi there, Marguerite's friend," he said.

Then I remembered. At the funeral—he had spoken to her and asked why she never came by anymore.

"Hi there, Marguerite's uncle," I said. I shocked myself, because it sounded pretty rude.

Luckily he laughed. "She's upstairs," he said. "Walk right on through. Second door on the right."

I walked up the stairs. There was a funny smell in the house. I couldn't bring it home—a kind of mishmash of blubbery cauliflower and toilet freshener. I knocked on the second door on the right.

"Yes?"

I opened the door.

"Oh, it's you." She didn't say it in a happy way or in a disappointed way. She said it just like that was the way it was, which is how it was, obviously.

"Yeah," I said.

I hoped she would say something, but she didn't. She was sitting on a bed with a yellow bedspread on it, picking at the fabric.

"I talked with Jaap," I said. "He thinks it's really too bad."

"Oh," said Rita.

"Shall I come sit beside you?"

"Why?"

Good question, why? I could go sit somewhere else, obviously. There were two chairs in the room, I noticed. It was one of those typical guest rooms where people put extra stuff, one of those rooms they never bother about. All the walls were white, ugly purple curtains hung in front of the windows, and there weren't any books or plants or other things that could have made the place a little cozier.

"It's a little easier to talk that way," I said. I didn't know if that was true, but it seemed like a good answer to me.

"It's okay with me if you go away," said Rita. "Why do we have to talk?"

Typical of Rita—why does she always have to ask such nasty questions? I didn't know what to say, so I said nothing, although I did sit down beside her (not too close).

"Are you angry with him?" I asked.

"It's okay."

Did I see it wrong, or was her lower lip quivering slightly? I realized I should say something nice, something comforting, something that would make her feel better. "It seems like a soap," I said.

A soap? What was that supposed to mean? I could have kicked myself. I looked at Rita. Would she start to cry? What was I supposed to do if she started crying? But she didn't cry. To my surprise, I saw the flash of a smile.

"Yeah," she said. "A soap opera. So, there's the camera and it's filming my face from really close up. And after that, your face. And you have to look really concerned."

"And then you're supposed to start crying, you know, those big, slow tears."

"Forget it."

We sat side by side in silence.

"What are you going to do now?" I asked.

"You know, go home in a while."

"Aren't you angry anymore?"

"No. Yes. I don't know. It bugs me that he never told me anything. Just fabricated stories."

"What kind of stories?"

"That's why I came here. I wanted to know what really happened. Now I know."

"But what did he tell you?"

"He was a skipper, way back. He brought ships from one place in the world to another. Okay, that was really true. He said that he met my mother when he was in Holland for a while. That was true, too, but the rest was all made up. He said it was love at first sight, forever, that he was overjoyed when she was pregnant and that he still had some sailing jobs he had to be away for for a time, but that they planned to get married and that he would look for a job on land to become a super-happy little family. And then my mother had that accident when I was a couple of months old. *Phew,* he always went on and on about my mother, that she was so beautiful and so sweet and so smart and so this and so that and so thus and so so."

Rita stopped talking for a moment to breathe. I realized I had never heard her say so many words in a row.

"While in reality he barely knew her," she went on. "Why make up all those stories? *That's* what bugs me."

"He thought it was terrible for you that you never knew her," I said. "It was all bad enough. He tried to make it a little less bad."

"He didn't even have a picture of her. Looking back, I don't understand why I didn't think that was weird. If you're totally in love and you have to go to sea for months, you take a picture with you, don't you?"

"Haven't you ever seen her?"

"I got a couple of pictures from my grandma."

"So, you *did* stay in touch with your mom's family."

"When I was little I did. But my dad couldn't get along with them, and I knew they didn't like him either. That's why I didn't go over a lot. Not at all the last few years."

"Obviously it was a real hassle with that guy she was married to—what's his name, Gerard—and with that lawsuit and stuff."

I suddenly realized I haven't written down that story yet. Jaap told it to me Saturday night. I shouldn't forget it, because it's a great story. (But there's so much going on that it's almost impossible to keep up with. I really have to start writing everything shorter.)

The door opened. Rita's aunt came in. "We're going to have lunch." She looked at me. "Do you want to join us?"

"Sure."

Rita's aunt left again.

"It's good material," I said. "We could make a movie about it."

"Yeah, right. You and your movies."

We went down to have lunch. Rita's uncle and aunt talked about everything under the sun but not a word about the situation between Rita and Jaap. They asked me hundreds of questions. I kept my answers as short as possible not to attract too much attention to myself.

"Do you know Rita from school?"

"No."

"Do you live close to her?"

"No."

"How do you know her, then?"

"From out on the street."

"Oh?"

"I'm staying with my uncle."

"That's nice."

If only they knew! Luckily they started talking about something else. "You're coming to the wedding, aren't you, Rita? He can come too." Rita's aunt nodded in my direction.

Wedding? What wedding?

"Janneke's going to get married Friday," Rita's uncle explained. "Our daughter. It's a little soon after the cremation, but Sara herself wanted it that way, she even said—"

"Oh yes, before I forget," said Rita's aunt, "we still have to make arrangements for the video. Pete can't really walk with that ankle yet. He says he can film just as well, but it doesn't seem like a good idea to me."

"Well, then Dirk'll just have to do it."

"Oh, please, no! You know how it went at Nathalie and Ber's wedding."

"Maybe we'll have to hire a professional," said Rita's uncle. "There's nobody else who's willing or able to film."

"What do you think that'll cost?" asked her aunt. "And then, on such short notice …"

That's when I had my brilliant idea.

"I'm willing to do it," I said. Where I got the nerve, I'll never know, but right after that I said, "for twenty-five euros."

There was a silence. Everybody stared at me.

"Are you sure you can do that?" asked the aunt.

"Does that mean you have a camera?" asked the uncle.

"Yes and yes," I said. "I have a camera and I've already made a lot of movies."

I thought of the takes of the neighbors' cat. They were really good. "And I really need the money."

"What for?" asked the aunt.

"You know, for stuff." I wasn't going to tell them what all was going on, of course.

"First, I want to see what you've filmed," said Rita's aunt. "It has to be a nice video, not a botch job."

—

To make a long story short (yeah, I'm learning): I went home and practiced shooting all Sunday afternoon. Tomorrow, I'll show them some footage. The wedding is Friday already. I have:

— The three old takes of the neighbors' cat

— Uncle Corry on the couch (short interview about angling and anglers)

— Myself, with camera (in the mirror: interview about making movies and what it's like being famous)

— Street scenes: a bus drives by, two boys are playing soccer, a man asks what I'm doing and why.

If I do a good job on that wedding video, maybe I'll get more jobs. Rita's got a very big family on her mom's side, and in big families somebody gets married at the drop of a hat or there's a so-manyeth-year anniversary celebration. I'll be able to earn loads of money. A shame that I'll have to spend it on going home and buying food and stuff instead of on cool things like a drum set. In any case, though, I'll be gone from Uncle Corry's and maybe I can make wedding videos at home, too, and earn money.

I wish my dad would come.

Tuesday, July 12

I was shocked as I was flipping through this journal just now and saw how much I'd written yesterday—not normal anymore. The book is already pretty full and I haven't even written everything down yet. A lot is about Rita and her problems, as if I don't have any problems myself. I don't really feel like focusing on them though. Things are already bad enough without my focusing on them. Meanwhile, Uncle Corry has become a faint shadow in the background. I hardly see him anymore. Either I'm out or I'm here writing.

Yesterday I went to see Tineke. I told her the truth. Suddenly the truth seemed a lot less terrible than at first. Well, it's still just as terrible, but that others know about it, I mean. Must be because of that whole Jaap-and-Rita business. Tineke wasn't angry at all, even though I'd strung up those lies about the Democratic Republic of Congo and stuff. Maybe it also helped that I told her the true story really pitifully and slipped in a lot of silences. She said I could always come by (just call first) if I wanted to talk or if there were any new developments and that I shouldn't think I had to face everything all by myself. "I'm here for you," she said. So, I asked if I could film her while she was working. It wasn't allowed. Too bad, I would really have liked to have her on film. Then I could have thrown out the Uncle Corry material.

I'm going to Weegbree Street in a minute (Rita's uncle and aunt's).

—

afternoon:

Rita's aunt was very stressed out. All kinds of things for the wedding still had to be arranged and she had totally forgotten that I was coming over to show my movie material.

"Just come back tonight," she said. "Then Arend will be here too."

"Arend?"

"My husband!"

That sucks. I walk halfway across the city to Weegbree and I can go do it *again* tonight, like I have nothing better to do. Well, actually I don't have much of anything better to do. I'm home alone right now because Uncle Corry is out fishing down on some canal.

I have a really weird feeling in my stomach. It's not really pain but something that comes close to it—kind of a semipain. Would it be punishment because I acted like I had a stomachache when Tineke was here (and when she brought me to the doctor)? I didn't tell her, by the way, that I was pretending. I didn't dare. It's also better that she doesn't know. What if I were *really* dying sometime and she didn't believe me?

I don't get why Uncle Corry doesn't have Internet or else a medical encyclopedia. I can't find out about anything, and I don't feel like going to the library because it's pouring rain out. Crap.

Suddenly I'm having all these thoughts about creatures in my stomach. They're devouring my intestines. Once I saw something on TV about a deadly disease where your whole body slowly gets eaten away by flesh-eating bacteria. It wouldn't surprise me one bit if I've got that too. This morning I noticed that all of a sudden, out of the blue, I had a wart on my knee. Crap crap crap! (And instead of those bacteria creatures eating the wart first—no, forget it, they're saving it for last.)

Just stood in front of the mirror in the bathroom for half an hour, bare naked. There's no mirror around in which you can see all of yourself (I can imagine Uncle Corry would rather not see himself all at once), so I grabbed a chair and inspected each part separately. My body has really weird shapes. I'll never believe it's normal. I also discovered a spot on my back. I can't remember ever having seen it before. It's still raining. And my brain sag is starting to come back too.

Do you know, by the way, what Corry told me about my mom Friday night when he was drunk? (Yes, of course you know that. I'm "you.")

(How ridiculous, really, some journal you write everything down in just for yourself.)

(If I started writing neater and crossing out some of the bad stuff, I could maybe make a book out of it.)

(But then, I'd use other names so nobody knows I'm me.)

He said that what had recently happened didn't surprise him at all, that she had always had strange tendencies.

"How do you mean?" I asked.

"Nothing was good enough," he said. "There were loads of boys in love with her back then."

"Really?" What a weird idea: in love with a mother (*my* mother!).

"But she thought they were all worthless."

"Well, maybe they were worthless," I said.

"And then she met your father. Suddenly he was good enough."

"Well, maybe that was true," I said.

"'Nothing but a helluva mess will come of it' was my first thought. And I was right in the end. Wasn't I?"

I looked at him angrily. What does he mean "a helluva mess"? *I* came of it. Is that a helluva mess?

He ignored my angry look. (He probably didn't even see it.) "She didn't want no construction worker, no policeman, no truck driver, guys who generally work for a living. No, wouldn't have 'em. They were way too low on the totem pole, I'm sure. But one of those artsy types ..." (he pronounced the words like there was something filthy stuck to it, shit or something) "... well now, that was suddenly good enough. I'm sure she found that interesting."

"Maybe it *was* interesting," I said. I tried to imagine my dad with paintbrushes in his hands and smudges of paint on his face, wearing funny clothes, with unkempt hair and all, the way you often see artists and characters like that look, but it didn't really work. I only knew him in normal clothes or in a suit and tie. I knew he'd been an artist before, of course, but he never said much about it.

"And then she got pregnant. Then she suddenly thought he had to go make money, have a career. Well, that's what he went and did—with that insurance whatsis, whatever it's called."

"And then? Was she satisfied then?"

Uncle Corry laughed loudly. "I about fell off my chair when I saw your father again a year later. He'd totally changed."

"And then?"

"Dunno. You guys moved. Hardly ever in touch anymore."

"Why not?"

"Just weren't. Your mother's got opinions about everything. People have to be like this and like that. I do everything wrong. She thinks I'm worthless." Uncle Corry got up and made a wobbly line for the kitchen. He came back with a fresh bottle of beer. "But now that she's in deep doo-doo, all of a sudden I *can* step up to the plate."

"How do you mean?"

"What do you mean 'how do you mean'? You're here, aren't you? And aren't I taking care of you?"

Well, if you can call it taking care of.

"Never a card or a jingle or whatever. Never inquires once in a while how things are. Even though I've been up the creek for two years with this back of mine."

Aha, so that's why he never works.

He picked at the label on the beer bottle. "Well, kid, you can't help it either. But they did make a real bassackwards mess of things."

Too bad I can't write down that weird Uncle-Corry-had-a-few way of talking. He spoke every word very distinctly and even paused between almost every word. If he didn't say such mean things, it might have been funny.

It's raining *again*. I'm wondering if tonight I'll still

My mom called! She asked how things were going with me.

"Fine," I said.

She said things were already a little better for her but that she still had to stay there for a while longer. She said she'd already called twice before but that I hadn't been in. That A-HOLE of an uncle of mine didn't even tell me about that!

65

I asked how long "a while longer" is, roughly.

She said she didn't know. I could tell by her voice that she was about to cry and was trying not to. I said it was kind of nice here and that I had already made some friends. Then she asked if I could put up with Corry a little bit.

"Sure," I said. "Everything's really okay. I've already got lots of friends here."

"That's good," she said. She sniffed some and blew her nose for a while. "I'm sorry it's all the way it is," she said when she was all done blowing.

"Doesn't matter," I said. "It's really okay here."

"Wonderful that you've already made some friends," she said.

"Yeah," I said. "It is wonderful."

"Do you need anything? Money or anything?" she asked. "Just tell me if you need anything."

"I don't need anything."

"If you need money, just ask Corry. Tell him he'll get it back from me later."

"I will."

"Make sure you do that."

We hung up soon after.

"So," said Uncle Corry. "She'll be staying there for a while longer."

I said nothing and quickly went to my cubbyhole.

I have the feeling my brain is expanding. It won't be long before it bursts through my skull. It feels a lot different than the sagging I had before. If I could choose, I'd prefer to have the sagging.

I'm not going back to Weegbree Street tonight.

Wednesday, July 13

I went after all.

I was lying on my bed, thinking, and suddenly all kinds of weird stuff started to happen. The walls got bigger and bigger and seemed to be really far away. The stacks of magazines, the windows, the curtains, *everything* got big and far. And now the scariest part—when I closed my eyes, the darkness was big and far *too*. How's that possible? Everything felt woolly and big and far.

When I got up and walked around, everything went back to normal. I didn't dare lie down again and decided to go to Weegbree Street after all. It was raining.

"So, let's have a look," said Rita's aunt. "The player's over there. Just slip the tape in."

It had been a whole ordeal to get from their front door to their living room. I was dripping, and dripping wasn't allowed on the carpet, only near the front door. Rita's aunt spread towels under me and on me. She rubbed my hair dry. I had to take off my coat and my shoes and socks too. She gave me a towel to sit on. I was finally in the living room. I carefully spread the towel on the couch.

"We're ready," said Arend (Rita's uncle).

That's when I realized I'd forgotten my camera and therefore the tape as well.

Rita's aunt sighed so hard that she could easily have supplied a whole hospital with oxygen. "Maybe we should ask Dirk after all," she said, "and give him alcohol-free beer on the sly. My word, a cameraman who forgets his camera. That doesn't bode well."

I really felt like screaming and yelling. Why is EVERYTHING, and I mean EVERYTHING, against me? (By the way, I did like the fact that she said camera*man* though.)

Arend was very nice. He said, "You know what? We'll just drive over to your house and pick the thing up."

That's what we did (after I'd put all my wet clothes on again). I sat in front. It was a very normal car and it didn't drive at all as nice and floaty as the cab. That was too bad. I should have checked the model because I don't want a car like that. Well, I'll do that sometime. I'll be seeing them often enough.

They looked at the scenes of the neighbors' cat while I looked at their faces. There was little to read on them. They looked doubtful when they saw the interview with Uncle Corry. I can understand that. Uncle Corry's not a joy, although they also looked doubtful when they were watching the mirror interview, even though that had been a really nice idea. After they had also seen the takes of the bus, the boys playing soccer, and the what-are-you-doing-and-why man, a silence fell. I didn't dare ask anything and waited until they said something. That lasted about an hour (or so it seemed).

"Hmm …," said Rita's aunt. "You *do* have a good camera."

"The colors are very good," said Arend.

"You don't have very much experience yet," said Rita's aunt.

"You're still a little young, of course," said Arend.

"You shouldn't move the camera back and forth so much when you shoot," said Rita's aunt. "Those images make me dizzy."

"I tried to make the images a little interesting," I said.

"What's interesting about slippers?" Rita's aunt asked. "Why, for heaven's sake, do you keep zooming in on that man's feet while he's talking?"

"Uncle Corry doesn't move much, and then it gets so boring."

"Corry?" she said. "Now what man would be called Corry?"

"I see some positive things, too, though," said Arend.

"What?" Rita's aunt and I asked at the same time.

"Uh ... well, that truck, for instance. It was nicely framed."

"Oh, was that a truck?" said Rita's aunt. "It moved so fast, I only saw a blur."

"I know how we can fix things up," said Arend. "Tomorrow, you go and shoot some more, but this time a little more calmly and a little tighter. Then, you come by again the day after tomorrow, and then—"

"The day after tomorrow?" cried Rita's aunt. "That's the day before the wedding. If he still can't do it by then, what are we supposed to do?"

"Then Rits will loan us his beautiful camera and we'll ask Dirk to film."

Rita's aunt sighed. "Oh, all right, go ahead."

Nobody said anything about money. I didn't dare bring it up.

evening:

This afternoon, Rita called. Could I come over? Crap. No, I thought, not just now. I'm not in the mood to keep having to focus on her problems. Anyway, I had to practice shooting. Typical of Rita, she never thinks that maybe I have things to do too.

So I asked, "Why?"

"I was thinking, and I've got an idea."

"Oh."

"And you can help."

"Oh?"

"See you later."

Jaap wasn't there. We talked about her idea and about other things. Jaap came home. I had dinner with them and am now here again because I still have to film. So, I don't have the time to write everything down.

All the time now, by the way, I hide my journal to play it safe. I put it in one of the stacks of *Angling and Anglers* here in the room, the big one at the foot of my bed, between the thirteenth and fourteenth magazine, counting from the top. Smart, eh? (I'm between thirteen and fourteen myself. That way I won't forget and I'll never have to look for it.)

Rita hasn't said a word, by the way. About her sitting here reading parts of it, I mean. I'm not going to bring it up myself, either, because then she might bring up the rest of what she read. I hope she forgets it. It really was pretty bad that she did that. I think it was stupid. A journal is meant to be read only by the person who wrote it. Maybe she has a journal or a diary and I'll go read it and then she'll know how it feels.

Thursday, July 14

Uncle Corry didn't want to be filmed anymore. He wanted to watch television. I suddenly had a brilliant idea. I called Rita and asked where The Geeks' drummer lived. Luckily she knew (he's a girlfriend's brother).

He lives near me. I went by and FINALLY something was working in my favor. He was home! And he was willing to be interviewed for the movie. He asked what it was for. "I'm a filmmaker," I said. "Who knows? Maybe they'll show this clip on TV someday. When you guys are famous, everybody will want to have it."

He thought it was a good plan. "Images from the early period," he said. "Sure. People always think that's a gas to watch."

Ha! I got to kill lots of flies with one stone:

— I got a good interview with an interesting somebody. (So, it's not so bad for the image not to move. It won't be boring like it was with Corry.)

— I got to know a real drummer. (Who knows? We might become friends and I might be allowed to borrow his drum set. Maybe he'll want to give me lessons for free, then, or for just a little money.)

— I was able to take advantage of the opportunity to ask him all kinds of stuff about music and the music industry. I'll already know a whole lot for when I'm a musician myself.

It was an amazingly good interview. I've watched it five times in the meantime (inside the camera, without sound, unfortunately). I almost can't wait to show it to Rita's aunt and Arend.

I don't have to write up the whole conversation because it's on tape, which I'll save of course. I posed really good questions, though, like if he liked drumming and what he's going to do with all the money when he's famous. I also held the camera without moving. After the interview, I filmed Danny behind his drum set (an old one, he said—his new drum set is in the rehearsal space). (Suddenly I'm thinking: maybe I can have the old one, or buy it cheap!)

Danny started drumming. He said he had to hold himself back and play quietly or else the neighbors would get angry. In spite of that it was totally awesome! Those neighbors really shouldn't complain. Anyway, it was more like they were bothering *us* because when Danny stopped drumming, they were pounding hard on the ceiling with something. So now those ugly *bonketybonk* sounds (not even with a sense of rhythm) are probably on the tape too!

Luckily I *do* have a sense of rhythm. That drum music is just totally contagious. I stomped along with my foot and kept the beat nicely. (The images in that part are a little shaky because of it, but I'll explain that at the presentation.)

In a minute, I'm going to go down the street so I can show that I can shoot all kinds of different situations tightly. At a wedding like that, obviously you've got all different kinds of situations too: city hall, the I-do, the bride and the groom arriving, the bride and the groom leaving, and so on. And then the party: dancing people, talking people, drinking people, cake-eating people.

9:30 (in the evening):
They're letting me do it! And if I do it well, I'll get twenty-five euros!

In my opinion, they were pretty impressed. During the takes of Danny, they looked doubtful again, so I expected the worst. That turned out to have mostly to do with Danny and not my shooting talent. The drum sound recorded really poorly, by the way. It didn't sound as good as it did live. It was all distorted. Made for a funny effect, though, together with the shaky images—really artistic. (I don't think Arend and Gea have a lot of artistic feeling though. They skipped that part!) (Turns out Rita's aunt's name is Gea. I figured that out because Arend, her husband, said that. He said, "Gea, is there any more coffee?")

Those people aren't easily satisfied. I'd done a beautiful take of an old lady behind one of those walkers with wheels, totally calm and tight, and they thought it was too long and boring! I said, "But I was supposed to shoot more calmly, wasn't I?"

"Yes, but showing how an elderly person shuffles along the sidewalk for half an hour is asking an awful lot of the viewer," said Gea. "It could definitely use some more action."

Yeah, yeah, yeah, it's never right. Anyway, it only lasted five minutes, tops.

On the other hand, they were really enthusiastic about my takes out on the square—children on the jungle gym, a man and woman kissing on a little bench (filmed from behind and not too long, it wasn't supposed to be a sex movie), and two puppies tumbling around. (That was a good move: Gea let out little cries and thought they were really cute.) Everything was filmed super tightly.

"All right, go ahead," said Gea. She sighed. "But just to make sure, we'll ask Dirk too. He'll just have to borrow Pete's camera."

"I'm sure it will be very nice," said Arend. "Twenty-five euros, wasn't it, Rits?"

Huzza, huzza! "Yes," I said.

"But if you botch it, you won't get anything," said Gea.

"Then Dirk will get the money?" I asked.

"Of course not," said Gea. "Dirk's my brother. He'll do it for nothing, thank you very much."

Ha! So, I'm the professional filmmaker and Dirk's the amateur.

I'll show them that it's very wise to hire a professional. That way at least you get a good product for your money.

I have to be at Weegbree Street tomorrow morning by ten o'clock. There's a whole program and I have to be at everything. (Am curious whether Dirk can be at everything.)

I should really go to bed but I don't think I can sleep. I'm much too excited. So I'll just keep writing for a while.

Rita has an idea. She wants to make a movie about her mom. It's a good idea in itself, but I think it should become *my* movie. It's *my* camera. I told her that too. "But it's *my* mother," she said. Finally we just decided that we'd do it together. If you ask me, though, she thinks *she's* going to do it now and that I'm helping her to film and stuff. I think it's the other way around, that *I'm* going to do it and that she's helping *me* to ask family members questions and stuff.

First, I'll just say (very quickly) what happened with her parents and her family, as far as I heard it from Jaap. It's totally one of those stories that would be easy to make a soap series about.

By the way, I want this story to be in the movie too—juicy story that'll sell well. I don't know if she wants to tell it on film though. Here it comes:

—

Rita's mom was called Anneke. Anneke was married to Gerard, some guy she had already known a long time. Anneke's whole family thought Gerard was terrific. (Why, I don't know. If you ask me, he was pretty boring and not very nice as far as I could tell from what Jaap told me about him.)

One day, she met Jaap, who was spending a week onshore. He was usually at sea because he brought these big yachts all over the place. That was his work. (Why those yachts have to be brought all over the place, I don't know, but he's been absolutely *everywhere*. Seems totally awesome to me! If I ever don't feel like being a filmmaker, maybe I'll do that.)

Something happened between Jaap and Anneke, something like—what's that called?—well, like, anyway Anneke was pregnant after that (but she didn't know it at first). Jaap went back out to sea. They agreed never to see each other again because Anneke was married and her husband, Gerard, wouldn't like it if his wife (Anneke) was running around with a sailor all the time. After a long while, six months or something, Jaap came back and then Anneke told him that she was pregnant. (She had a really fat belly by then, so you could see it, too, I would think.) She didn't want to tell Gerard. (I don't get that, because he could *see* she was pregnant, couldn't he??? Or maybe he thought she'd eaten too much?)

Meanwhile, Jaap left again to bring a sailboat somewhere. He was pretty shocked by the belly. That belly wasn't what he'd had in mind.

Gerard found out, too (had he been blind up to that point?), and he didn't like it. He got angry and wanted a divorce. Then the whole family found out and everybody got mad at Anneke and even madder at Jaap (even though they didn't even know him!).

Other than that, I don't know exactly, but in any case Rita was born and a couple of months later her mom had that bad accident and died. Jaap wasn't there at the time, and Rita's aunt (I don't know which one) took care of Rita for a time.

After that there was a lot of hassle and even a court case about who would take care of the baby (Rita). Jaap said he was her father and therefore should take care of her, but Anneke's family said he was a rotten bum and that *if* that were to happen, it would be over their dead bodies, and that Jaap didn't have a leg to stand on because Anneke had been married to Gerard when Rita was conceived or something (I don't know what that has to do with anything), blah blah blah. On top of that, it was *his* fault that Anneke and Gerard had divorced, and Gerard was such a good man and Jaap was a big asshole (this last isn't true at all!). All kinds of lawyers got involved and it cost a bundle too.

That's more or less how it went, if I understood it right. Jaap got what he wanted, but the whole family still despises him. Well, it's all really complicated, and I'd better not get any more involved. Besides, it's incredibly long ago and I don't understand why they're still making a fuss over it.

So, anyway, now Rita has a plan all of a sudden to make a movie about her mom. (Actually it was *my* idea, but it seems she's forgotten that. When *I* thought it up, there in her aunt and uncle's guest room, she acted like it was a really stupid idea!) She wants to go to all her family members to interview them. She already wants to start tomorrow, at the wedding, because everybody will be there, even the aunts and uncles who live far away. I said, "Well, that's out because I have to film the wedding." (I didn't know that for sure yet, but I was, of course, hoping I was going to.) She didn't like that, but I stuck to my guns! Yeah, a whole new Rits was standing up, self-confident and sticking to his guns. That wedding video is really, really important. I'm being paid for it!

"I'm sure you don't have to shoot *everything*," she said. "In between the other stuff, you really will have time for another movie."

"Well, if I have time," I said. "Maybe, but I'm not promising anything."

"You'll have plenty of time," she said.

Actually I think it'll be kind of cool. I'll be making two movies in one day! I'm sure there aren't too many filmmakers who can do that. I bet Dirk never managed to do that.

Then Rita suddenly started talking about something else. "So, where are *your* parents?" she asked.

That's not exactly what I'd been waiting to hear.

"And don't start in about the heart of Africa, because obviously nobody's going to believe that."

I kept my lips sealed. She certainly doesn't need to know everything about me.

"Well? You know everything about *my* parents now. Tell me something about yours. Where are they?"

"I don't know," I said.

"What do you mean you don't know?"

"Somewhere in India, I think, but I'm not sure."

"Oh, just stop telling those stories."

"It's true."

"How's that?"

"The last card I got from my dad came from India. That was over a month ago. Maybe he's gone somewhere else again in the meantime." (Maybe he's even in the Netherlands, I thought after that. Maybe he's even looking for me.)

"What's he doing there?"

"All kinds of stuff."

"Sailing?"

I TOTALLY didn't feel like talking about it, but Rita can be really pushy. So I told her briefly that my dad had quit his job and then decided to travel. About the girlfriend and stuff, I didn't tell her (or Tineke either). I'm pretty sure Rita now thinks that he's there with my mom, and I'm just going to leave it at that. She doesn't have to know everything.

I thought it was a nice opportunity, as it happens, to ask her something that had been bothering me for some time already. She's always asking me hundreds of questions, so I thought I should be able to ask her something.

"Don't you have any girlfriends?" I asked.

"'Course I do."

"So, where are they?"

"One just moved and one's on vacation. Why are you asking?"

"I was wondering, like, well, I think it's kind of unusual that …"

"That what?"

"The day you went to buy cigars for your dad, you took me to the store and then I had to come over right away that night. How come, though? You didn't know me at all."

"Like, you know."

"What do you mean?"

"I was bored."

That's nice. So, it wasn't because she thought I was cool or nice but because she was bored.

"I was totally bored out of my skull."

Go on. Make it even worse.

"Karin had just moved. Lisa had gone on vacation. I had nothing to do."

"Don't you have any hobbies or anything?"

"'Course I do, plenty. Swimming, for one. But on your own, it's not as much fun. And listening to CDs all day or reading books gets old real fast."

So, might as well pluck a Rits off the street. Sometimes I think she's not cool at all, that girl, but I wasn't going to say that right then, of course. I don't want to get into a fight with her just before the wedding, or else maybe she'll work up her aunt against me and I'll be fired.

Well, I think I'm going to try and sleep anyway. Tomorrow's an important day—my first day as an official filmmaker!

Sunday, July 17

evening:

Phew, like what a bunch of stressed-out people they are, especially Gea. If the whole family's like that, I'm not sure I still feel like doing any more on that movie about Rita's mom.

Luckily Pete *is* cool (but he married into the family, isn't real family). Pete is also an uncle of Rita's. Usually *he* films everything that has to be filmed in the family, but he has a sprained ankle at the moment.

We worked really well this afternoon, and Pete said that it had every possibility of being a nice video when he's done with it. Very handy, that editing thing of his. You can cut and paste all the images and put them in other spots and work on them. You can do just about anything with it, even edit and mix in images from different movies. You can see an obvious difference though. The images I made have much better color than Dirk's. Pete said so too.

I think those people have *very* little feeling for art. They only want that boilerplate stuff. But isn't it boring to film the bride and groom the WHOLE time, while that official guy goes on and on about everything under the sun?

I even said to Gea, "Now I'm totally lost. You thought the sequence of that old lady with the walker lasted way too long. It was boring. It could use more action, you said."

She starts hysterically yelling at me that I'm a stupid moron and that she's even more stupid because she let me shoot the movie. (She said a whole lot more besides.)

Now, I ask you, is it me? Does what that woman says make

any sense? One time she says this, another time that. And by the way, the I-do *is* on it. I can hear them both clearly say yes, both of them. So, what difference does it make if you don't see them for an instant? You see them long enough the rest of the time, just like the boring official.

But okay, so at any rate Pete stuck in one of Dirk's takes in that spot. It had to be done, I guess, because they made a whole lot of hoopla about it. Now you see weird color differences though. On top of that, Dirk filmed them from behind, so you see just their backs. I thought my images were much nicer (birds outside in the tree, tight zoom on Eva's face) (Eva = Rita's cousin). What is nice is that you see me for a second, too, in Dirk's takes. You see me while I'm filming.

Rita thought it *was* a good movie, by the way. She had to laugh really hard when she saw it. (I let her see some choice parts yesterday morning, in the camera, without sound.) Rita obviously has a better understanding of that kind of thing.

How can I help it that those people have no taste? It already started with the bride's gown. Looking back, that might not have been very bright on my part. It just hadn't occurred to me, though, that when I whisper something to Rita while I'm shooting, my voice is going to be recorded too. (Pete already took that out, by the way. You don't hear me anymore. Now there's some music.) The bride really did look like a cream puff though! (Pete said so, too, this afternoon, said I was right.) Oh well, a lot more of that kind of stuff went on, too much to write all of it down. In any case, it's nice of Pete to help—even though the movie's not going to look as nice and it'll be a lot more boring. Those people really want it to be as ugly and as boring as possible, so I guess it'll have to be that way. I do hope that take ("shot" it's called, says Pete) of the coat closet stays. I think it's great, with all those raincoats and umbrellas. According to Pete, a shot like that isn't really necessary in a wedding movie, and definitely not a shot that's so long.

No matter what Gea says, I think I have real talent for being a filmmaker. Pete also thought I have nice ideas. He did say that some of those ideas weren't really all that appropriate for a wedding video, though, and he gave me some good tips. For instance, people would rather see faces in a movie like that than legs and feet the whole time. (It wasn't the whole time, just fifteen minutes.) I thought it was a fun idea, not so boilerplate. And when you shoot from the floor, you can get under tables and stuff too. People don't see you then, so they talk really differently than when they *do* see you filming.

Gea's face when she heard some of those conversations on tape! (In comparison, the cream puff thing wasn't even so bad, I think.)

Rita keeps acting stupid all the time. She says that I'm in love with Eva. Eva is her cousin. That's not true at all (that I'm in love, I mean, that she's a cousin is. Pete is her dad.). She's pretty cool, but I'm really not in love or anything. She just looked nicer to film than most of the other people at the wedding and I wanted to make a good video, not a boring one with nothing but old people.

Really childish anyway—Rita is sometimes a real teenybopper. That's when you do notice she's four months younger.

Uncle Corry's back with the french fries.

9:05 p.m.:
I wonder if french fries really are healthy. Uncle Corry says they

are. He says they're potatoes and potatoes are healthy. You always hear, though, that french fries are not healthy and that they give you pimples. At home, my mom sometimes gets french fries, too, on Sundays. She says you shouldn't eat them every day, but now and then can't hurt.

I'm a little worried about those pimples. I didn't think of that until after I'd already emptied the container. Just looked in the mirror to check, but there was nothing to see yet. Uncle Corry says he's going to try to go back to work, but that it'll be hard with that back of his. He can forget about construction work. (That's what the doctor told him.) I said maybe he could sail, bring sailboats from one place to another, but he didn't think much of that. It would be impossible with his back, he said, running around hauling and lashing ropes all day, on top of which you need at least a hundred diplomas. (Really? I'll have to ask Jaap.) And then, the idea of all that water and the same view every day didn't appeal to him. I don't understand what difference that makes, seeing as he already has the same view from his couch every day and I never hear him complain about that.

I'm a little tired. It's been pretty busy the past few days, with all that filming and stuff. I'm going to bed early. Tomorrow morning we're going swimming. (Hope it doesn't rain this time and that the water's a little warmer.)

Monday, July 18

5:10 in the morning!:
I can't sleep anymore. I've been lying in bed, awake, for an hour already. I wish those birds out there would shut up! How come there are birds in a city? Let them go to the woods or something, somewhere where they won't bother us. I don't go and twitter under *their* tree and keep them from sleeping.

I don't know Mrs. B the neighbor lady's number. How do I get it? I'm worried about our house. When I went to Uncle Corry's, Mrs. B said I shouldn't worry, that she would water the plants and whatever. What's the situation with the rent though? Who's paying it? What'll happen if the rent's not paid? What about the other bills? I want to go over there. Maybe there's a card from my dad there. She said she'd send my mail on to me, but maybe she forgot or lost Uncle Corry's address. I haven't received anything yet. Why wouldn't my dad send a card? Soon, the rent won't have been paid and other people will suddenly be living there who *do* pay the rent. Soon, my dad will come home and other people will be living there and he'll ring Mrs. B's doorbell to ask where I am and she won't be there or be dead. She's old already. Does my dad still remember where Corry lives? He doesn't know anything about where my mom is and stuff, so he can't call her to ask.

I'm going to call Mom.

They said it was still too early. I said it was important. They asked what was the matter. I couldn't come up with anything fast, so

I said I couldn't sleep. They said I should call back in a couple of hours. I felt tears coming on, but I didn't cry. Maybe I should have. Maybe I would have gotten her on the phone then.

Nobody said anything more about the twenty-five euros. If I had that money, I could go by train. I'm going to ask Arend. I don't think it's fair if I don't get the money. If I don't, I'll ask Corry. He'll get it back later sometime. I don't feel like swimming.

± 4:00 p.m.:
We swam.

At nine o'clock I called again, but she was busy doing something and really couldn't come to the phone right then, they said. I'd just have to call back later. They were willing to tell her that she should call me when she was done.

"Do that," I said. But then I remembered that I was supposed to go swimming and that she was sure to call when I wasn't in, so I said, "Never mind. I'll call back."

Then I called Tineke. She wasn't there yet (at work).

After that, I went to Rita's and we went swimming. She thought I was quiet. I said I'd slept badly because of those rotten birds.

It was nice weather luckily, but I thought the water was still too cold.

We talked about our film. Actually Rita did most of the talking. I don't really feel like making that movie anymore. Rita acts like it's all *her* movie. She's come up with all kinds of stuff. I didn't feel like coming up with things. She's also come up with a title: Anneke. If you ask me, I could come up with a much better title, but I don't feel like it.

I just called Tineke again. She was there. I'm going to see her tomorrow morning.

My mom didn't call. I'm not going to call her anymore today. I'm just not in the mood right now.

Tuesday, July 19

Pete wants to help with the movie about Rita's mom! When we've interviewed everybody and done all the takes, we can put it all in the right sequence and edit it with him. He can also stick photos in and add music or a voice that says something. It's going to turn into an awesome movie!

We also talked about showing it. We'll invite the whole family as well as friends of Anneke's.

"Even Jaap?" I asked.

"Who knows?" he said.

"What about Gerard?"

Pete's face took on a strange expression. (He didn't say anything.)

I suddenly remembered that we really should interview Gerard. He knew Anneke for a long time. He was even married to her, so I'm sure he can tell lots of juicy stories about her. Or would he still be angry?

Pete and I cracked up over Dirk's wedding reception shots (the ones taken later on that night).

"This is exactly why Dirk can't borrow my camera," said Pete. Pete has a really good one, even better than mine. (Maybe I'll even be able to borrow it for the movie about Anneke.) Dirk must have dropped the camera at least four times while it was on. Made for some funny shots though.

"Remember, Rits," said Pete. "A cameraman should *not* drink alcohol." Like I was ever going to do that!

—

Pete wanted Eva to let out Dachsy, the dog. (It's not a dachshund at all. It's one of those black mop-haired dogs you can clean the floor with.)

I said, "Oh, cool. Walking the dog."

"Why don't you go too," said Pete. "Stretch your legs. I'll keep working."

"I don't feel like it," said Eva, and then to me, "Why don't you go if you think it's so much fun?"

"Uh …"

"Go ahead," said Pete. "I'll be fine on my own for a little while."

So, minutes later, I was walking through the neighborhood with Dachsy. I passed Gea and Arend's house (by accident). They live nearby. Of course Dachsy just *had* to sniff the streetlight in front of *their* house at length (for at least an hour and then pee gallons). I tried to kind of hide behind the lamppost so they wouldn't see me. I remembered that I really should ring the doorbell and ask for the twenty-five euros, but I didn't dare. I peeked inside from behind the streetlight. They were watching TV. If Arend had been alone, I might have dared.

Do you know what I saw in their house (in Pete's house, I mean)? A cross! It was hanging on the wall. Are they Christian? I don't know any Christians. But if *they're* Christian, wouldn't the rest of Rita's family have to be Christian too? I don't get it. As far as I know, there's no cross hanging on the wall over at Arend and Gea's. (Gea and Eva's mother are sisters.) Did they pray? Gea and Arend didn't do that. I ate over there and they didn't say grace. Or don't you do that when it's just sandwiches? Maybe they only do it for warm meals. I'll ask Rita.

Once I'd seen the cross, I was scared they'd suddenly start praying or singing songs about God. I don't know any songs about God.

Saw Tineke this morning. I told her I was worried about the house. She said she was sure something had been arranged. Rent is often paid automatically from a bank account.

"But what happens when there's no more money in the account?" I asked.

She didn't know.

We sat at her computer and looked for Mrs. Bolman's (Mrs. B's) phone number on the Internet so I can call her. Tineke said I should also give my mom a quick call and that she was sure there was nothing for me to worry about. I told her that I couldn't ever get her on the phone. She said that maybe I should ask the people over there at what times it was best for me to call. My mom often had things to do there, obviously, so she couldn't come to the phone. But she would also have free time at some point.

Suddenly she gave me a little package. "Present," she said. I opened it. It was a cookbook. It was really meant for my uncle, she said. Maybe he didn't like cooking by himself, though, so then we could do it together. That was more fun than doing it alone.

The book's called *Tasty & Healthy: Creative Cooking for Beginners.* I've already read some of it. There are all kinds of tips in it about eating healthy, and then there are recipes in it so you can easily make a (healthy) meal. "In no time," it says.

I don't feel like giving the book to Uncle Corry at all. I also don't feel like cooking with him. I wouldn't mind cooking on my own, but then I'd have to have money to buy groceries.

—

5:30 p.m.:
I got money for groceries! Uncle Corry didn't make a fuss about it at all. I'm going to make spaghetti with sauce.

evening:
Finally finished doing the dishes and cleaning up. They don't say a thing about washing dishes. "In no time," it says, but they don't say that after that you'll be busy for over an hour getting everything clean again, not just dishes and silverware. The pots are the worst (particularly that one pot), not to mention the rest. There were red spatters all over—on the cupboards, on the floor, on the counter (and on my clothes, but that's not so bad).

Except for that funny little taste, it was pretty good. Uncle Corry said I shouldn't have turned the burner up so high, that's why it burned. If he knows how to do it so well, why doesn't he do it himself?

There aren't a lot of tasty things in *Tasty & Healthy*. (It makes me wonder if all that "healthy" stuff is true.) They write a lot about meals made with some kind of cabbage, with green or red cabbage or sauerkraut or cauliflower or kale.

Tomorrow I'm going to make macaroni for a change.

later:
Called Mrs. B. No postcard had come. If one did, she would send it on. She still had Uncle Corry's address. There were no other people living in our house. It seems the rent's being paid.

I just looked at my dad's postcards again. There's one from Australia, one from Indonesia, one from Sri Lanka, and one from

India. I thought about how long it was each time before a new postcard came. I think about a month, never longer, although now it's been a lot longer than a month since I got the last card. Had something happened? Maybe he has no time to send cards. Or maybe he's in a really poor country where they don't have mailboxes, although India's a poor country and it seems they have mailboxes there. Tomorrow, the library.

Wednesday, July 20

My dad's got a line! I discovered that this morning when I looked at the atlas over at the library this morning. You can draw a straight line with your finger from Australia to Indonesia to Sri Lanka to India. If you continue it, you come to Iran, Iraq, and Turkey. On the map, Turkey's a lot closer to here. So, I'm sure he'll come home really soon. He's probably not sending any cards because he's already on his way. You can even draw the line all the way to the Netherlands (by way of Hungary, Austria, and Germany)! I didn't have a ruler, so I laid another atlas along the line so that the line was completely straight. That's how I could tell that he is going through Iraq in fact, through Turkey, and then through Europe.

I showed Rita the postcards this afternoon. Actually it's kind of cool. I've got a dad who's been in all those countries. So, I said, "Look, he's been to all these places, plus Iraq and Turkey, and now he's somewhere in Europe, in Austria or Germany, I think."

"My dad's been there too," she said. "And to lots of other countries besides." I'd forgotten about that.

I told Rita that I had discovered the Australia-Netherlands line. We looked at the world map. (It turns out Jaap has a really nice atlas.)

"The Middle East," she said when my finger was around Iran-Iraq. "There's always war there."

"Not all the time, I bet," I said. "And I'm sure my dad isn't going to go straight through a war. He'll make a detour."

"Then it's not a straight line anymore," said Rita.

I wish Uncle Corry got a newspaper. There are papers at the library, but then I have to go there every day.

By the way, I flipped through the atlas a bit more and came across Africa. What did I see? The Democratic Republic of Congo doesn't even exist! Not in Jaap's atlas anyway. The country is called Zaire there. I don't get it.

Rita asked why my dad was traveling and where my mom was (she had figured out by now that my mom wasn't with him).

"I don't know exactly," I said (why my dad is traveling, I mean). "He didn't like his work anymore. He didn't feel good."

"What exactly did he say?"

"Nothing."

"Nothing? He just left, without saying anything?"

"He said he didn't like his work anymore. He said he didn't feel good."

"I'm sure you've noticed, haven't you, Rits?" We were sitting at the kitchen table. He had asked if I'd sit down for a minute. "That things aren't going very well."

I hadn't noticed a thing.

"Parents would be better off just honestly telling their kids what's going on—because kids have antennae. They always notice."

I hadn't noticed a thing.

"I'm not feeling very well. My work … I hate my work. Your mom … Well, I'm sure you've noticed it all. So, it's better that I live somewhere else for a while."

"Where, then?"

"I don't know yet. I'll first just go and then we'll see."

He left. Later it turned out he was with that girlfriend and stuff and that he had been living there for a while. Then, he suddenly called for me to come by. He told me that he was going on a trip with that Florrie woman.

"Where to?" I asked.

"I don't know yet. We're just going to go, then we'll see."

"When are you coming back?"

"I don't know yet. I'll send you lots of postcards so you'll always know where I am."

He's sent four up till now. Is that a lot? I don't know.

I didn't feel like talking with Rita about it, so I started up about the movie. (Comes in really handy, that movie. Now I can stop any conversation I'm not in the mood for by starting to talk about that movie. It's her favorite topic.)

I asked he

My mom called!

She asked me how things were. I said things were fine. She asked if I needed anything.

I said, "No, I don't need anything. I've got everything. I made a movie."

She liked hearing about that. "Good for you!" she said.

"It's a wedding video," I said. "It's almost finished. It's going to be really good."

"A wedding video? So who got married?"

"Janneke. That's Gea and Arend's daughter. Gea and Arend are Rita's aunt and uncle. Rita and I are also making a movie about Anneke. Anneke is Rita's mom, but she's dead. We're going to interview everybody: Eva's mom, because that's Anneke's sister, and of course Gea, because she's her sister, too, and Dirk, because he's her brother, and a whole lot more family members and friends. I hope Gerard, too, because Anneke was married to him, so I'm sure he has a lot to say about her, but I don't know where he lives, and maybe Jaap, too, that's Rita's dad, but he didn't know Anneke very well, so maybe we won't interview Jaap. And Pete's going to help with the editing and stuff. That's when you stick the images together in the right order. Pete is Eva's dad, he's married to Eva's mom and Eva's mom is Anneke's sister, but you already knew that because I already said it."

"Oh," said my mom. There was a silence. "You already know a lot of people over there. I'm happy for you." I heard her sniffle a little. Why was she sniffling?

"Yeah," I said.

"Very happy," she said. "Honest."

There was another silence.

"Do you ever think of me?" she asked.

"Yup," I said.

"Don't think of me *too* much though."

"Nope."

"Just sometimes, just for a minute, so you won't forget me completely."

"I won't."

"I think of you a lot, too, and then I wonder if you're all right over there with Corry."

"Everything's fine."

"I'm happy to hear that."

"Mom, what's the deal with the house?"

"What do you mean?"

"Is the rent being paid? And the other bills?"

"Don't you worry about all that."

"I'm not worried. I've just been wondering about it lately."

"Everything will be all right. I don't want you to worry."

"I'm not worried. Are you going to have to stay there long?"

"I don't know exactly, a little while yet. Can you handle it for a little longer?"

"Sure, things are going really well," I answered. "I can cook. I made spaghetti with spaghetti sauce. And tonight I'm making macaroni with macaroni sauce."

"Good for you!"

"And I can make cauliflower, too, and sauerkraut and green cabbage and red cabbage. So, when you come back, you won't have to cook all the time. I'll be able to do it."

She said I was a sweetheart. She would call again very soon.

As I was hanging up, I remembered that I hadn't asked at what times I could call *her*.

Maybe it's better for me not to call her, though, because maybe she'll think something's wrong and that things aren't going well. I don't want her to start worrying.

evening:
Uncle Corry said it tasted good. He ate two plates (of macaroni, not the plates)!

We ate really late, though. I didn't feel like shopping and cooking because my brain was bothering me. I don't understand why sagging brain isn't in the encyclopedia. I thought I should probably go see that doctor again soon so I could ask.

I was lying on my bed and having all these thoughts. I imagined I had to get an operation on my head. First, they open it all with a saw and then they do all kinds of things, like placing your brains in the right place again and maybe cutting certain parts out that aren't good anymore.

And then, while I was thinking, something really scary happened. I saw spots in front of my eyes that danced up and down. After that, everything got hazy, with half-see-through spots. I couldn't really see the room anymore. My head felt really weird, like there was too much air in it, and now I know FOR SURE that I have sagging brain. And, like that's not bad enough, maybe I'm going blind too.

I feel really rotten for my mom because she's already got so many problems and then on top of it all, she'll have a blind son with a sagging brain.

I lay on my bed for two hours all in all, but then I thought I'd better get up to eat healthy. Who knows? Maybe it'll go away by itself if I eat well, with lots of vitamins, and that operation won't be necessary. At the library, I'm going to look up what kinds of vitamins I have to eat for healthy brains and eyes.

When I went shopping, I already felt a lot better. So I think I won't go to the doctor after all. Otherwise maybe he'll start asking questions, and I don't feel like being asked questions. On top of that, maybe he'll say that I need an operation. First, I'm going to see if I can manage to get better by eating healthy.

I don't understand what's with Uncle Corry though. He's acting totally weird. He put a cookie tin on the counter and stuck some money in it. "For groceries," he said. "Then you won't have to keep asking for it. Just take what you need." He's suddenly being a lot nicer. He seems almost normal.

We talked over dinner—at first mostly about eating. He said that he didn't like to cook. I said that maybe I wanted to become a cook someday. (I don't know about that yet. First I'll have to see how things go with making movies.) He didn't even laugh at me. He said that it was a good idea. It was better than going into construction because you could get back trouble doing that, he said. Other than that, construction was pretty good. Making things with your hands. He did miss that nowadays.

"When you cook, you make something with your hands too," I said.

Corry thought cooking was more for women. I didn't understand that because he had just said that he thought it was a good idea for me to become a cook.

"Yeah, but then it's work," he said. Excuse me! I really don't see the difference. And why would cooking be something for women anyway? Men can do it just as well. I can, at least (and my dad can too).

Then all of a sudden I asked why he didn't have a wife. It just came out. In fact, I didn't want to ask that at all because it pretty much makes sense. Just try to find women who would want to be married to Uncle Corry. I'm sure that if they had a choice, they'd prefer not to be married to him.

"I went out with somebody for a couple of years, but it fizzled out," he said.

"Oh." I wonder what kind of woman she was.

"She was always badgering me."

"Oh yeah?"

"I wasn't allowed to do this and wasn't allowed to do that, but then there were all kinds of things I did have to do. You know how that is."

"Yeah," I said. (I have no idea how that is.)

"Other than that, she was a nice gal. But she was always badgering me."

So that's when he said that it was tasty. The macaroni, I mean. He dished up seconds and then the pan was empty.

Friday, July 22

I've been here for three weeks to the day. Pretty long already, but it seems even longer, like months. When I see how much I've written, it's like I've been here a year already.

Rita wanted to start with her aunt Gea. I didn't think that was such a good idea. I wanted to start with Alied (Eva's mom's name, or so I heard from Rita). She started in again about my being in love with Eva! I said it had nothing to do with that, I just wanted to wait until Gea had cooled off some about that wedding video.

"Aha! So you *are* in love," said Rita. "You admit it."

"Not at all! What gave you that idea?"

"You just said so yourself. You said that it had nothing to do with *that*. So it's true."

I just about exploded.

"She won't want you anyway," she went on. "She only likes older guys, boys of fifteen or sixteen."

"What difference does that make to me? I'm NOT in love!!!"

I wondered how Rita could know that. About the older guys, I mean. She barely knows her cousin.

"I talked with her for a long time at the wedding reception."

Huh? Could she read minds or something?

"She asked who you were."

Oh yeah?

"She said you kept filming her, so she asked. That's why."

"Oh."

—

We had already tried to interview some family members at the reception, by the way, but nobody wanted to do it. It was time to celebrate, they said. They didn't feel like talking about Anneke now because it would make them sad. Some other time.

Only Dirk was willing. Dirk is a totally happy guy. You couldn't make him sad if you tried. Dirk lives nearby, though, so we could interview him later.

Went to Pete's again last night. The wedding video is almost finished. Pete worked on it while I wasn't there. I didn't like that, but he said he didn't have a lot of time and it was faster to do it on his own. I don't understand. I happen to think that I really help and have a lot of sense for what shots really have to be in it (except he doesn't think so a lot of the time, and usually he gets his way).

We went to the room where he keeps his video gear, sat down, and suddenly he said, "The mother-thing, Rits."

I was surprised. Why had he said that? What did he know about my mother?

"Where's the mother-thing?"

Did he think I didn't have a bond-thing with my mother? I started mumbling something about how things hadn't been going well with her but that it was better now and that she called a lot and I called her and that we ...

Pete gave me a really funny look. "The tape," he said. "The videotape with the edited sequences."

Huh?

"The master. I was calling it the mother-thing."

"Oh, okay," I said. My cheeks burned red hot. You could easily have fried two eggs on them. I frantically dove in among the tapes that were strewn all over the table and pretended to look.

"Oh, here it is," said Pete. "I found it." He put the tape into the player, but instead of getting to work he leaned back in his chair and gave me a searching look.

"You've got quite a few problems, isn't that so, Rits?"

"Not too bad," I said. Crap. I was so glad that I talked about nothing but movies with Pete and that he never asked difficult questions.

"It's good to talk about them sometimes."

"I do. I talk about them a lot."

"Where is your mother anyway?"

"Oh, like, you know. In uh … well, there. She has to be there, uh … but she'll be coming back really soon."

It was quiet. He kept looking at me. "And your father?"

"He's traveling. He'll be coming back really soon too."

"Do you feel badly abandoned?"

I wanted to say that that wasn't the way it was, that I was at my uncle's and he was taking care of me and that things were going really well, but it didn't work. It felt like there was something stuck in my throat, a stone or a rock-hard potato. The words wanted to come out, they pushed as hard as they could, but they couldn't make it past.

Why should I feel abandoned? I don't feel like I was abandoned. It would be weird if I felt like I'd been abandoned. My mom can't do anything about it. She honestly didn't do it on purpose. And my dad didn't know this was going to happen, or else he really wouldn't have left on his trip. So, he can't do anything about it either. They didn't abandon me, because abandoning somebody is something you do on purpose and they hadn't done it on purpose, so why should I feel like I was abandoned? I didn't like Pete saying that. I feel rotten about it, that's true, but, honestly, not like I was abandoned.

I wanted to say all that, but because of that stupid potato rock, it didn't work.

Then Alied (Eva's mom) came in with coffee for Pete and tea for me.

We worked for two hours and when we were done, he started in again. "It's good to talk about it, Rits. Everybody needs support. Nobody can do it all alone."

"Yeah," I said. Suddenly I got an idea. "I need money. I was supposed to get twenty-five euros from Gea and Arend for the wedding video, but I haven't gotten anything yet."

"Really?" said Pete. "Well, just leave that to me. I'll make sure you get it."

Ha! Now I didn't need to go to Gea myself to ask.

"Why do you need money?" asked Pete.

"You know, for all kinds of stuff, the train and stuff—then I can go home sometime—and also to buy healthy food." That last bit wasn't true because now I had the cookie-tin money, but Pete didn't have to know that. If I were to say I needed money to go live on my own in my own home, for sure he wouldn't think that was a good idea. Grown-ups always think kids can't take care of themselves, even though there are plenty of examples that they can. Just look at Remi in *Alone in the World*. He had a bunch of bad situations to deal with, a lot more even than I do, but he managed. He had a dog though. That might make a difference. I read the book a couple of years ago. I still remember that back then I thought: Remi isn't all alone in the world. He meets lots and lots of people, nice ones too, *and* he's got his dog. (It was still really sad sometimes though.)

"You'll also need tapes to record your film about Anneke," said Pete. "They cost money too."

I hadn't even thought about that. "I've got the tapes with the wedding shots," I said. "I can record over them when the film's done."

"Don't they belong to Gea and Arend?"

Oh yeah.

I'm also suddenly thinking now that we'll need money for the train to go see family members who live far away. If you ask me, it'll never work out with that film. Soon I'll have twenty-five euros, but that won't be enough by any means for all the tapes we'll need for filming *plus* the master tape *plus* the train tickets.

Who knows? My dad will come back soon and I'll get the money from him. Maybe I can ask for a year's advance on my allowance.

I wonder what will happen if he suddenly comes back now. I keep thinking we'll just go live in our old house, but maybe it won't be like that at all. Maybe he'll go live with that Florrie woman again and I'll have to stay here. I don't want to live at Florrie's. She has a tiny house full of junk and weird stuff.

She was really nice to me, though, the time that I was over there (when my dad told me they were going on a trip).

"This is Florrie," my dad had said. "A good friend of mine."

Florrie had shaken my hand. "I'm Florrie," she had said. "A friend of your dad's."

For a long time, I thought that she was just "a friend" of his (like Rita's a friend of mine, say). Only much later did it turn out that they were involved with each other—dating, having a relationship, or whatever it's called when you're talking about parents and people like that. I only discovered that when I came home from school one time, though, and wanted to make myself a sandwich and once again there weren't any plates. Later I saw them, broken, in the trash, and I asked my mom what had happened. She said she had had a fit of anger and that's why she had smashed all the plates against the wall. Only then did she tell me what was going on with my dad and that Florrie woman, even though she'd already known it for a long time. (My dad had been gone for over two months by then.)

I'm going to make some rice, with vegetables and peanut sauce.

evening, 11:00 p.m.:
I have an awesome idea!

I was sitting on the couch next to Uncle Corry—I didn't feel like doing anything, so I was watching television with him. Uncle Corry always wants to watch local TV. I don't know why. They're totally boring programs. (Oh, maybe that's why. Uncle Corry himself is, of course, totally boring.) This time I was glad about it though—that that's what we were watching, I mean. They were showing a piece about an animal shelter with money problems. The cages had to be fixed up. A couple of people had organized a sponsored marathon. That's when a bunch of people run a long race and other people or businesses give money for the run. They gave the money to the shelter. The marathon was called

Running for Animals. They had run for over two thousand euros altogether. The shelter people were really happy with it. "Thank you, on behalf of the animals as well," said the lady who was the head of the shelter. The animals themselves didn't look happy or thankful though. The cats sat in their cages, staring out sourly, and the dogs looked ticked off, but that's not the point. The point is that I suddenly had an awesome idea.

I'm going to look for sponsors for the movie about Anneke! If all of Rita's family members (which are a lot) give twenty euros or more, say, then we'll have money for videotapes, for train trips, *and* I'm bound to have a lot left over for myself! Then when the movie's done, I can go home. Maybe I'll even have enough to buy a drum set.

I called Rita right away, but nobody answered. I can't wait to tell her the plan.

The rice came out pretty well, I think, except I put a little too much hot sauce in it. It made it so you couldn't taste the dish very well. My lips and mouth were on fire! Uncle Corry drank three bottles of beer during the meal (to put out the fire, he said), and I must have had five glasses of water. Now Uncle Corry is at the café down the street.

Funny, though, it doesn't matter at all that I'm at home alone. I'm not scared or anything. Soon, I'll be home alone *all the time* (when I'm home, I mean), and I don't want to be scared all the time then.

Saturday, July 23

Everything was going so well.

Jaap and Rita were totally enthusiastic about my plan. Jaap said he would start helping us right away by giving us not only some money but also some stamps so we could write all the family members about the sponsorship thing. We got started writing the letter. Jaap said that I was a resourceful fellow, a real businessman. All afternoon, I walked around with a happy tickle in my stomach.

Until I got home.

There was a postcard from my dad. He's not in Austria or Germany. Not even in Turkey. He's in Memphis, in the U.S. Line's gone. He doesn't have a line at all.

Why did he have a line at first but not anymore? Maybe he's not planning to ever come back.

He writes, "Hi there, Rits. The Mississippi is beautiful. Memphis is beautiful. Everything is beautiful. Maybe to Mexico after this. It's beautiful there too, they say. Greetings from your dad."

It's all beautiful, just beautiful. I feel like throwing plates around the room.

I just pelted about twenty *Angling and Anglers*, one after the other, against the wall. Doesn't have much effect though. Plates are probably better, but I don't feel like getting them. I've so had it. Just when everything seems to be going better, something happens that makes everything worse again. I'm not in the mood for the movie anymore. I'm not in the mood to write anymore. I quit. It's all useless anyway. Nothing's worthwhile.

Sunday, July 24

Video camera: Rita
   €25: animal shelter
   Toys and clothing: children in poor countries
   Bicycle: Steven
   Books and comics: hospital
   Cookbook *Tasty & Healthy*: Uncle Corry
   Journal: in coffin
   The rest: Mom and Dad (split between themselves)

Maurits Frederik Hofmeijer

Monday, July 25

Spent a long time this morning with Tineke. I told her everything, including about my dad and that Florrie woman and that he's probably never coming back. I also told her about my sagging brain and all those other things. I talked for a long time without stopping and she said nothing. She just looked at me with eyes that were sometimes big and sometimes even bigger. Only when I was talked out did she talk. She said a lot. I'll write it up in short.

— That I'm bothered by a sagging brain does not mean I'm going to die. It can just be tension that makes my head feel bad.
— Sagging brain doesn't exist. She had never heard of it (although that might be because there's nothing about it in the encyclopedia).
— If I'm worried about my health, I should just go see a doctor. A doctor can reassure me that I'm not going to die. Tineke's willing to go with me.
— My dad will come back absolutely for sure. That he doesn't have a line doesn't mean anything. You're on the other side of the world in no time by plane. The States is just a few hours of flying time.
— I have to try not to have thoughts about *when* he's coming back. It could be a long while yet (but maybe not). If I have thoughts, I'll be disappointed if things go differently than I expect.
— If he comes back before my mom, that still doesn't mean I have to live at Florrie's house. I can choose to continue staying with Uncle Corry for a while.

— If I'm still at Uncle Corry's when vacation is over, I'll have to go to school here for a while. Tineke will help me with that.

— It's very normal to feel abandoned. It's fine for me to be mad at my dad (for instance).

— You can be angry with somebody and still love that person.

This is a really short version of everything she said. I must have sat with her for two hours. She even called off another appointment!

Pete finished the wedding video. I was supposed to see him yesterday, but I called to say I was sick. Last night, he called to say the movie was ready and that when I'm better again, we can go to Gea and Arend's to let them see it. (Janneke and Simon aren't around. They're on their honeymoon.) I just called to say I'm better. We'll go tonight. Rita's going too.

Tuesday, July 26

I got the twenty-five euros.

The video turned out really well—super tight. Even Gea was satisfied. It's too bad that a whole lot of nice shots aren't in it anymore, but, like Pete said, the client is king. That means that the client is the boss and can say how he (or she) wants it to be.

When it was over, Rita and I didn't feel like going home. We went to the square and sat on a bench and stayed there so long that it slowly got dark. There were stars. We talked.

Rita said she didn't really miss her mother because she never knew her, even though she did miss "a mother," if I got her meaning. Her girlfriends had mothers and then she saw that it was nice to have one. She also had a girlfriend who had no father, which she, on the other hand, did have—a really awesome one even, more awesome than most fathers she knew.

I asked why Jaap had never married. That way she could have had a new mother.

"I don't know," she said.

It was quiet for a time. I thought of Florrie. What if my mom has to stay there for always? Then Florrie might be my new "mom"—a kind of second mother. Would she wash my clothes, then, cook my food, help me with my homework, care for me if I were sick? She doesn't even know me and I don't know her either.

"What are you thinking about?" asked Rita.

"About my dad," I said. "I got a card."

"Are your parents divorced?" she asked.

"No."

"So, they're together?"

"Uh … no, not really."

"What are they, then?"

"They're still married, but they don't live together anymore."

"Are they going to live together again?"

"I don't know."

We looked at the stars.

"The Big Bang," said Rita. "That's how it all started."

"What?"

"The world. The universe. First, there was nothing, then there was a bang, and then all this was here."

"How can something come out of nothing?" I asked.

"I don't know," said Rita. "That's why some people believe in God instead of in the Big Bang. They say that God made everything. Otherwise it's impossible, they say."

"But where does God come from, then?"

"No clue. Maybe God's always been there."

I tried to imagine "always." Can something have always been there? It must have started at some point, right?

"Maybe God started with the Big Bang," I said. "And made everything after that. That way, everybody's right: the people who believe in God and the people who believe in the Big Bang."

I thought of the cross on the wall at Eva's house. I had wanted to ask Rita about that, but not now.

"My dad knows a whole lot about the stars," she said. "He knows exactly what they're all called and where they are because he sailed a lot. Look, see those stars over there?"

"Yeah."

"You just think you do."

"What do you mean?"

"Their light has traveled for millions of years before it gets here. Those stars you think you're seeing already went somewhere else a long time ago. Some of them don't even exist anymore. They've exploded or whatever. But the light that they once shone from that spot is only now reaching Earth."

"Millions of years?"

"Yeah. Or trillions, I don't remember exactly. A whole bunch anyway."

I thought of the cards from my dad. They also traveled for a long time before they got here. Maybe he had meanwhile gone somewhere else again a long time ago. Maybe he didn't even exist anymore.

"The card from my dad came from the States," I said.

"Really? So, he went the other way?"

"I don't know which way he went—not the right one, at any rate."

Then I told her about Florrie—and about my talk with Tineke.

"If you stay here, you should go to my school," she said. "We'll make sure you're in my class."

"Okay," I said.

"But what's with your mother? Where is she?"

I told her a little about the plates and stuff and that her nerves were on edge and that it kept getting worse instead of better. "She needed rest," I said. "So, she had to go somewhere where it's very restful."

"You mean on vacation?"

"Uh … yeah, kind of a vacation."

"So, when is she coming back?"

"When she's rested. I don't know how long that's still going to take."

"And you'll be staying at your uncle's until then?"

"Yeah, or until my dad comes back—except if he's going to live with that Florrie woman again. I don't want to go there."

"I think your uncle's a weird guy. I think I'd rather live anywhere than live with him."

"He's not so bad," I said. When I had said that, I suddenly thought it wasn't a lie. He's gotten a lot more normal lately, less dumb and ornery and nicer too.

"If Florrie were to live with Corry, then everything would be solved," said Rita. "Florrie and Corry, that sounds good!"

I imagined them together and had to laugh. "I don't think she'll feel like doing that."

"Florrie and Corry were made for each other. They belong together. Corry and Florrie, couple of the year!"

We cracked up. Rita even rolled on the ground.

"I think it would be pretty cool if you were in my class," Rita said as we were walking home.

Later on in bed, I realized I didn't feel as rotten as before.

We're going swimming in a minute. I asked Corry if I could use the cookie-tin money to have an ice cream or whatever. (At first, I wanted to do it on the sly, but that didn't seem like a good idea after all.)

It's okay with him. Now I don't have to touch my twenty-five euros.

± 6:15 p.m.:

Eva went swimming too!—along with Dachsy.

We mailed the sponsor letters first. There were fourteen. We had the letter ready and printed it a bunch of times and put it in envelopes, but then we had to have all the addresses. Jaap didn't have them. So we went to Pete's house. Eva's mom had all the addresses.

We said we were going to the pond and then Eva wanted to come too. Pete had an old bike, by the way, that I'm allowed to borrow as long as I'm here. Then I won't always have to walk or sit on the back of Rita's bike. It doesn't ride at all as nice as my own bike at home, but I'm pretty happy with it.

We were a really cool little club, Eva and Rita and me and Dachsy. We ran into Danny the drummer, and he sat with us for a while. Then we were an even cooler club: Eva, Rita, me, and Danny (and Dachsy).

Danny asked if I wanted to film a Geeks performance sometime. I said it would cost twenty-five euros. He didn't want me to do it after that. I said everybody pays that and it's not much at all for a good video, but Danny said he'd ask somebody else, somebody who'd want to do it for nothing. Then, I said we could negotiate the price, but that videotapes cost money, no matter how you look at it. Danny said not twenty-five euros, though. I said making videos is work and the band doesn't play for nothing either. They get a lot of money to do that. He said the pay was pretty good, so, okay then, he'd pay ten euros, but no more. I said okay.

Eva and Rita listened to our conversation. If you ask me, they were pretty impressed with how professional I was. Danny told us the CD recording wasn't going so well. They keep arguing while they're recording, particularly one guitarist and the bass player. The guitarist will say, for example, that the bass player's playing weird things or making mistakes, so he gets confused. But the bass player says that the guitarist just has to listen better and not just be into himself.

Then, the singer (who's also the other guitarist) argues with Danny and says Danny has to drum differently. And Danny in turn thinks the singer has to sing differently. That's why they now want to have a live take to hear how they play live. During performances, things *do* always go well, said Danny. Then they hardly ever argue. And they'd like to see themselves for once while they're playing. That's how come the video.

It seems to me like making music's pretty hard. Seems like you have to pay attention to a lot of things. You can't just do what you feel like doing, and you'll quickly get into arguments. I don't really like arguments.

After a while, Danny got up and said, "Well, kids, I'm going back to my friends."

"Kids?" Rita cried. "Yo, who are you talking to?"

Danny laughed and walked away.

"Old fart!" she called after him.

Then Rita and Eva started whispering and giggling (really weird, a giggling Rita). They didn't want to say what they were whispering about—really pathetic.

After that, they went back to acting normal, luckily, and it was fun again.

I beat Eva and Dachsy at who could get to the other side fastest.

(Rita beat me, but that doesn't count because she swims faster than anybody or anything.)

I'm going to cook something easy because it's pretty late and I still have to go shopping.

Wednesday, July 27

9:30 in the morning:
Last night I made pancakes. The cool thing about doing your own cooking is that you can decide what you're going to make. In *Tasty & Healthy* there are all kinds of variations on pancakes, so the food's not only tasty, but healthy, too, with vitamins and stuff. You can roll pancakes up with spinach inside, say, or homemade applesauce. Homemade applesauce I'm going to do some other time. This time I just bought a jar. The first pancake burned. I had the burner on too high. The second pancake was a kind of slab, it was that hard. I had the burner on too low. (Uncle Corry said the thing fell under the weapons act. You could easily commit a murder if you clobbered somebody over the head with it and brained them.) After that, my pancakes came out well.

I asked Uncle Corry why he didn't have a dog.

"Dogs are filthy animals," he said. "They're covered with fleas. They stink. They shed."

Now he was talking just like my mom.

"A dog's nice to be with," I said. "You can walk with it. You can go swimming with it. You can do just about anything with it."

"And you have to take it out every day. Three times at least."

"You're never alone if you have a dog. If you have a dog, there's always somebody at home."

"They bark your ears off. They're dirty animals. They think so in China too. They eat dogs over there."

I imagined Dachsy broiled on a spit or chopped into pieces and mixed with rice. "Why do they eat dogs if they think they're dirty?" I asked. "You don't eat what you think is dirty, do you? That doesn't make any sense."

"*We* eat pigs. They're dirty too."

"I think pigs are cool." I decided never to eat pig anymore. "There are a lot of dogs at the shelter," I said. "We could easily take one of them."

Corry didn't think it was a good idea though. I'd be gone soon and he'd be going to work (he hoped) and then the dog would be here alone all day.

"So, I'll take it with me," I said. "When I go home."

Corry laughed. "I know your mother," he said. "I know her very well. You might as well forget it."

"Maybe I'll be living with my dad," I said.

"Really?"

"Depends. Maybe."

And here it comes: "That's maybe not such a bad idea," he said!!!

Why did he say that? Doesn't he think my mom's a good mother? I didn't like him saying that.

"It doesn't surprise me one bit," he went on. "I always wondered when the whole business was going to bust up."

The business? What business?

"That head of hers. It's full of weird kinks. And, well, now we know."

My mouth was full of pancake so I couldn't ask him what he meant exactly. I wasn't sure I really wanted to hear it either, but he went on of his own accord.

"She's always got to have everything perfect. But nothing's ever perfect. Life is full of shit. That's the way it happens to be.

Can't change that. But not as far as she's concerned, no, she just acts like that's not how it is. Shit doesn't exist where she's concerned. Everything's all organized and perfect. Should have seen her room when she was a kid. You could've eaten off the floor, so neat and clean. I wasn't allowed to set foot in there of course. I wasn't perfect enough."

She is awfully neat, that's true, but aren't all mothers like that?

"And your father, he had to be perfect too. No, it doesn't come as a surprise to me at all. Maybe they can take a couple of those kinks out of her head over there. But a dog, no, forget it. You'll never manage."

Now that I'm writing this conversation, I'm thinking about whether it's true. Does everything have to be perfect for her? What is it, perfect? At home, everything was always just the way it was. No idea if that was perfect. My mom was the way she was. My dad was the way he was. And I was ...

Hmm, what *was* I anyway? Probably I was just the way I was too. I don't know. I never thought about it before. Suddenly, though (a lot more of late), I'm thinking maybe everything was different than it was. Maybe it wasn't the way it was at all.

Well, that's okay. It all sounds too complicated. I can't even understand myself anymore.

Tonight I'm going to make brown beans, a kind of variation on chili. I wanted to do that before. I think brown beans are pretty good, but Uncle Corry says he doesn't like brown beans (he likes the white ones though). I couldn't care less. He'll just have to eat what I make and not complain.

———

In that letter, by the way, we didn't ask for twenty euros or more. I wanted to, but Jaap thought it was better to leave it up to everybody what they wanted to give. He said, "You just have to explain that you two need some money for this film, for the cassettes, the train tickets, and other expenses, and say that you'll both be happy with anything they would like to contribute. Otherwise, it'll seem like you're begging, and people don't like that."

I'm afraid that a lot of people will give only one or two euros. Why would they give more if they don't have to? I'm afraid I won't have any money left over.

I'm going to think about other ways to get some. I'll be earning ten euros with that Geeks movie soon, but then I'll have to spend it to buy videotape.

I'm going to the library.

evening:

I looked at the map. Memphis is in the southern United States, on the Mississippi River. In which state Memphis is I couldn't figure out. There are all those vague dotted lines and Memphis is right on the border of one of those lines. If you go all the way down along the Mississippi, you get to the Gulf of Mexico and by then you're really close to Mexico. It could well be that he's going farther down after that, to South America. You've got a lot of countries there. If he goes there, I'm sure it will take a long time before he comes back. South America's pretty big. I'm sure there's a lot to see in all those countries.

In Mexico, they often eat bean dishes. That's what it said in *Tasty & Healthy.*

Uncle Corry complained about the brown beans. I said, "Then make your own food." He didn't have anything to say to that. He emptied a whole plate and then said they weren't so bad. It would stay down, he said.

"But Ah ain't goin' ter pray fer 'em."

"Huh?"

"Ah ain't goin' ter pray fer no brown beans." He laughed loudly.

I asked what was so funny.

"That's something from a while back," he said. "Little Bart."

"Little Bart? Who's Little Bart?"

"It's a TV series. Everybody used to watch it."

Little Bart was a country boy from Drenthe who thought brown beans were disgusting, Corry told me. He didn't want to say grace and pray for them. He didn't think that was necessary for something as gross as brown beans. He'd shout, "Ah ain't goin' ter pray fer no brown beans," and then his parents would be furious and they'd let him have it.

"Brown beans are pretty good," I said. "And besides, I don't get it. Why do you have to pray if you don't feel like it?"

"We always had to say grace too," he said.

"You guys? You mean you and Mom?"

"So, when we had brown beans, I'd mimic Little Bart, and my mother'd get angry and I wouldn't be allowed to watch TV for a week."

Pray? I couldn't believe my ears. You do that only if you're a Christian, don't you? I didn't know that my grandpa and grandma were Christians. So my mom is too. She never said anything about that before!

I've been writing way too long again. I keep trying to write everything shorter, but I can't. Everything's just as long as it is. From now on, I'm going to try to write more often so I don't have to write so much all at once. Time to go to bed.

Thursday, July 28

It's Eva's birthday. On Saturday, she's going to have a party and I'm invited! She called Rita to invite her and she said I could come too. (I was just on the phone with Rita.)

Now the only problem is that I have to buy a present. I have no clue what to buy, plus no money. Well, I do have some money, but I don't really feel like touching it, although I do want to have a good present to give her. I'm going to ask Uncle Corry for present money.

later:
Uncle Corry turned his back to me and said, "Just pluck it off."
Me: "Huh?"
Him: "Go on, pluck it off!"
Me: "What?"
Him: "The money."
Me: "I don't see any money."
Him: "Oh no? So, it's *not* growing on my back? Gee, well then that's too bad for you." He laughed loudly.

Crap. I thought he'd changed a little, but that's not true, I guess.

later:
I got some money! (I'm super smart!!!) And I also know what I'm going to give her. I suddenly had an awesome idea. I'm going downtown now to buy it (handy having a bike) and tonight I'll write about my smart idea to get money from Uncle Corry. That can't be written really short and I'll have more time then.

—

later:

I bought something else. All the books about stars were too expensive, but this is really nice, too, and it's wrapped really nice.

later:

Maybe she'll think it's stupid. I don't know if I'm going to give it to her. Maybe I can still exchange it for something else. But what?

later:

I'll give it to her, I guess. I don't know what else to get. I'll just tell her that she can exchange it if she thinks it's stupid.

later:

I can't find the receipt. I thought I put it in my pants pocket but it's not there. What now?

evening:

Maybe I can work in a restaurant instead of here in the kitchen to earn money. At this point, I can make almost everything there is to make (except the disgusting things, but I don't want to make them). Tonight: boiled potatoes (peeled them myself), peas (frozen), and cheese soufflés (also frozen). Uncle Corry said he'd rather have a pork chop than a cheese soufflé, but I said he'd just have to make it himself. I don't really like big meaty things, and I don't feel like cooking for everybody separately. (On top of that, I think it's sad for the pig.)

Uncle Corry said there was supposed to be gravy on potatoes

or else they weren't fit to eat. I didn't have any gravy though. The potatoes were a little dry, it's true. So I put mayonnaise and ketchup over them. That was good. Corry thought so too. "Good idea," he said.

I'm also thinking up new recipes. I've got real talent. Who knows? Maybe I'll write a cookbook or, better yet, present a cooking program on television. That way I can combine all my talents: making films and cooking. (Somebody else will have to run the camera though. I can't do everything at once.)

Uncle Corry said my mom had called while I was downtown. She was going to call back soon. She must have said something about having to stay there for a while because he suddenly started in about my cubbyhole. "Maybe we should make it look a bit smarter," he said.

"Smarter?"

"Smarten things up," he said. "Maybe you'll be here for a while yet. Wouldn't you rather have a smart-looking room?"

Smart-looking? "Well, maybe we can make it a little cooler," I said.

"How?"

Give me a break. He started in about it himself and now *I'm* supposed to come up with everything. "You know, paint it or whatever. A couple of posters. A plant. And put away those *Angling and Anglers.* Then there'll be more room."

"Put them where?"

"In a closet. Or throw them away."

Throwing them away he thought was a bad idea, but he would look to see if he could find another spot in the house for them.

"Then there will also be enough space for, like, a computer," I said. "That looks smart, a computer."

"You sit in there a lot, so I thought, if we just spruce things up a bit ... What do you do in there anyway?"

"Like, you know, read or write or think about making movies."

"What do you write?"

Why was he suddenly so interested? I realized I'd quickly have to start hiding my journal somewhere else. I don't want him to find it when he starts cleaning up the *Angling and Anglers*.

"Like, you know, a book," I said.

"A book? About what?"

I couldn't make anything up quickly, so I put a big piece of potato in my mouth and mumbled something. I couldn't even understand what I was saying, something in a kind of foreign language.

"What was that?"

"Woowo, avou vah," I said with my mouth still full. I thought now he'd stop asking about it, but no.

"What? I didn't understand a frigging word of that."

I swallowed and at that moment I got a smart idea. "About my parents," I said. "The book's about my parents." Now I'd have a great reason to ask him questions if I wanted to know something. He's bound to give a normal answer if it's for something important like a book. (Lots of times he gives me those stupid answers when I ask about something.) (Lately he hasn't been too bad about that though.)

I believe he thought it was just weird to write a book about your parents. "What the heck's there to write about?" he asked.

"I wouldn't know what to write about *my* parents. It would be a skinny book. One page or something."

"If you ask me, there's plenty to write about," I said. "You told a story just yesterday, about those brown beans. That's cool to put in a book."

To Uncle Corry, it didn't seem at all cool to put in a book.

By the way, it occurs to me I'm getting smarter all the time. Maybe that's because I've been eating lots of carrots lately. I don't like cooked carrots, so now and then I buy one of those bags of carrots that have already been cleaned and I eat a bunch every day. Uncooked, they go down. I read in a library book that there are vitamins in carrots that are good for your eyes. (Aside from the sagging brain, I've been having trouble with my eyes lately.) That's when I got the idea that they are probably good for your brain, too, because it's right near your eyes.

So, this afternoon I thought of a SUPER SMART way to get money from Corry for the present. Here it comes: I flopped down on the couch beside him. "I don't think I'm going to cook tonight," I said. "I'm probably not going to cook at all anymore."

"Oh?" said Corry. "Why not?"

"I thought about what you said the other day."

"What did I say?"

"That cooking's more for women. I think you're right. So, it seems to me it's better not to do it anymore." I got up and slowly walked toward the door. "If it were work, of course, I *could* do it. If it's work, then it *is* something men can do. Don't you think so?" At the door, I turned to him for a second. "It's too bad, because, of course, something is work only if you get paid for it." I walked out of the room to my cubbyhole. Ten minutes later he was already standing at my door.

"You'll get ten euros a week," he said. "Here." He gave me a ten-euro bill. VICTORY!!! My first cooking pay!

I also know what I'm going to say from now on to those people who always ask you what you want to be someday: "Nothing. I don't have to be anything someday because I already *am* everything I want to be. I'm a cameraman and a cook and earn loads of money." They'll do a nice double take at that, those people who always ask you what you want to be someday.

Friday, July 29

I think it's pretty rotten for Uncle Corry. Soon, when I'm gone, there won't be anybody to cook for him. He won't get any vitamins at all anymore, just like before. I was thinking about that this morning in bed and I had (another!) good idea—except I don't know exactly how to go about it, but that'll come.

Sunday, July 31

Eva said that it's not fun to have a birthday during summer vacation because lots of her girlfriends are always gone. She said I was
lucky, since that's why I could still fit in the van.

Very funny. Otherwise she wouldn't have invited me at all!
Right away I didn't feel like giving her my present anymore. The
good thing was that I didn't care so much anymore if she thought
it was stupid or not. (I never did find the receipt.) She said she
thought it was cool. She already had a diary, she said, but it was
almost filled and this one was also really beautiful, with a cool
little lock on it and all.

I wish my journal had a lock on it. Then I wouldn't have to
worry. I'm hiding it under my mattress now because Uncle Corry
might come and clean up the *Angling and Anglers* any minute.

Eva's parents (meaning Pete and Alied) had rented a van that
could fit a whole lot of us. We went to the zoo. Girlfriends of
Eva's came along and another woman, Petra (that's Eva's mom's
best friend). I didn't know any of the kids, but that didn't matter
because Rita was there too.

Eva acted so busy and attention grabby the whole time—
totally girlish. (Rita said so too.)

Rita and I walked with Pete and Alied and Petra a lot. At least
they acted calm. Now and then I heard them sigh when, ahead of
us, Eva went into her theatrics again.

"Little kids are fun," said Pete.

"Too bad they grow up," said Alied.

They laughed.

When we were looking at the elephants, they told us it had been really hard to come up with something to do. Eva had thought everything was stupid and childish. Only the zoo she thought was fun. "Okay, we'll do that then," they had said. "But that means only a couple of kids can come, otherwise it'll cost too much." In the end, it had turned into six anyway (plus the three grown-ups) and they had had to rent a van. Eva thought six kids were "not a lot."

My mood improved after this story. Eva hadn't invited me *just* because there happened to be a seat.

There are incredibly many different animals at the zoo. (Well, that makes sense obviously.) Sometimes it made me dizzy. Rita and I saw a blind girl with her parents. She had one of those red and white canes. We wondered what's fun about the zoo if you can't see anything. So, we took turns playing blind-kid's bluff, where one of us covered their eyes with a jacket and had to tell the other one what there was to experience and where we were without seeing anything. That was lots of fun. (I'm happy, though, that I'm not blind *all* the time because that doesn't seem like fun to me at all.)

We kept getting it wrong. When I thought we were at the seals we were at the hippos. When we really were at the seals, I could smell it. It smelled really strongly of fish, except I thought that we were at the polar bears then.

There are lots of sounds at the zoo and lots of smells too. Now I understand better that a blind person can have fun there, too. The elephants really smelled like elephants, the lions smelled like lions, and the zebras smelled like zebras. They all have their own smell (although you do have to know which smell belongs to which animal).

I was pretty tired when we got back. Some of the kids had to go home. A couple stayed to eat pancakes. (I did too.)

Now I had a fine opportunity to compare! And you know what? My pancakes taste just as good as Pete's, maybe even better. I said I can make pancakes, too, and that there are all kinds of pancake variations, like with spinach or homemade applesauce rolled inside.

"Mmm, homemade applesauce," said Alied. "I'm going to make some again soon too."

"Yuck, no," said Eva. "It tastes much better from a jar. That kind doesn't have any pieces of junk in it."

(If I make applesauce myself, I'll have to make sure there aren't any pieces of junk in it. I don't like pieces of junk either.)

Only when all the pancakes had been eaten did my eye fall on the cross on the wall again and I realized that they hadn't said grace. Maybe they don't pray for pancakes, though, only for beets and red cabbage and that kind of thing. Maybe you need more support from God then.

This afternoon we went swimming again. (Eva, Rita, and I. Dachsy didn't come along.)

I've got a plan! And that plan has already been put into action, although I'm still holding off on writing it down because I first want to know for sure that it's going to work. What if a certain someone accidentally found my journal and read about it?! If it doesn't work, that someone won't have to know.

Monday, August 1

in the evening:
This afternoon I waffled for a long time in the journal store. It won't be long before my book's full. So I have to get a new one. At first, I wanted to buy one just like the one I gave Eva, because it's got a lock, but they look so girlish and they're small. Mine is a lot bigger and thicker, and they had journals like that in the store, too, but they don't have locks on them. I don't get how those girls do it with those little books. Maybe they don't go through much, or maybe they write in really teensy-weensy handwriting.

I'm going to wait until next week to buy a new one. Then I'll have new cooking pay plus the ten euros filming pay from Danny. (I already bought the videotape.) Danny called last night. He had gotten my number from Rita. Would I be able to do it Saturday? They're doing a gig then. I can.

I hope there won't be so much going on for a little while so I won't have to write much. Otherwise, I won't make it till next week.

Tuesday, August 2

I figured out how long I've been here now. I've been here exactly 1 month and 1 day. I came here on a Friday night. That was July 1. Figured in weeks, I've been here exactly 4 weeks and 4 days. (Hey, what a lot of 1s and 4s!) Figured in days, I've been here exactly 32 days.

Last night I stopped writing to save writing space. Instead of writing I started thinking. I believe I'd rather write though. Thinking always gets so complicated after a while. When you write, it all seems a little simpler and less complicated.

I started thinking about what Uncle Corry said before about how he'd be able to write only one page about his parents. That made me think about what kind of stuff *I* might write about my parents if I were really doing a book about them. I actually couldn't come up with a whole lot either.

After that, I tried to remember my life. I remember all kinds of things, but no important or interesting things (well, until a couple of months ago, that is). That's when I started worrying about the movie about Anneke. What if nobody knows anything interesting about her? Then it'll be a really short movie and really boring. Maybe then everybody will want their money back. It would have been handier to make a movie about Rita's dad instead of her mom. At least Jaap has done interesting things, but then, Jaap's not dead. That's too bad. Well, of course I don't mean that. I'm happy he's not dead. It is handier to make a movie about somebody who's done interesting things though. *That's* what I mean.

Then I started imagining that my parents had disappeared, in, like, the Democratic Republic of Congo or in Zaire, and that I was going to make a movie about them. I realized that I wouldn't know a lot of people to interview. A few friends, a few people from my dad's work, sure, but besides that, no family or anything. Yes, Uncle Corry, of course (but he usually talks about not-cool things and I'd rather have cool things in a movie like that), and my dad has a half brother, but he lives in Australia. I don't know him.

I wish I had a big family, like Rita does. There's always something to do in big families, like a birthday or a wedding. And everybody knows everything about everybody, so you can ask about everything. I don't think I'll be getting a big family anymore, though. I wouldn't know how. I don't understand why my parents don't have any more kids. Well, there was that little sister, but she died right away, so I never knew her. It seems as if everybody dies before I get to know them—not just that little sister but also my grandma and grandpa and my other grandma and grandpa. Other kids have a mess of fun grandmas and grandpas, but I have nothing. And since I've been here, an awful lot of people died before I got to know them: Anneke, Rita's aunt (Sara, from the funeral), and maybe a lot more I don't even know about.

So, I tried to pray. I asked God, "Please give me a large family. Seems like lots of fun." But, well, we're not believers at home (not that I know of, at any rate), and I had no clue how to go about being one exactly. So I think praying was pointless. In any case nothing happened. It also seems like it would be hard to arrange, even for God. The way it is with my parents now, I don't think they want a whole lot more children. And then, they're old already too. Say, how old can you be and still have kids? Phone's ringing.

—

My plan's working! Rita (she just called) said it had been a big hassle, but it worked out. Now I just have to tell Uncle Corry really carefully. I don't know, maybe he won't think it's cool at all. Maybe he'll even get angry. Maybe, though, he'll think it *is* cool and be happy. I have to find a way to tell him so he'll think it's cool and not get angry.

later:
Maybe it would be better for me not to tell him, not yet at least. Otherwise, he might say he doesn't want to. I'll just tell him Friday night, right before he goes to the café. Then he won't have any time to get angry or say that he doesn't want to.

evening:
I'm finding it hard to act normal with him. It's starting to be noticeable. He asked, "Why are you smirking like that? Is something up?" I hadn't even realized I was! I'm going to Rita's in a minute. I want to know exactly what they said. (We couldn't talk about details on the phone because Corry was around. I said I'd stop by tonight.)

Wednesday, August 3

I'll have to tell him earlier anyway—in fact today even. He has to buy new clothes and go to the barber and stuff. Rita said it would be a waste of time if he didn't do that. Petra looks pretty good. If somebody looks pretty good, that person will prefer to go out with somebody who also looks pretty good.

In any case, they have a date. Of course, Uncle Corry doesn't know that yet, but Petra does. (Petra is one of Eva's mom's friends. She went to the zoo with us.) (Oh, I already wrote that. Oh, well, doesn't matter.) Petra's advantages:

— She's not married (was, but not anymore).

— She has no boyfriend (had one, but not anymore).

— She would very much like to have a boyfriend or a husband.

— She can cook.

(Eva knew all of this. I questioned her when we went swimming Sunday.)

So, that works out just right. If things go well between her and Uncle Corry, I don't have to worry anymore about nobody being around to cook for him soon. She can go ahead and do that.

Everything had to happen in a roundabout way. Rita called Eva and Eva called Petra. At first, Petra didn't want to. She said she didn't like blind dates. (A blind date has nothing to do with being blind. It means you have a date with somebody you've never seen before. So you do keep your eyes open during the date and you don't put a jacket over your head either.)

—

It was hassle enough though. It cost me a lot of effort before I convinced Rita to convince Eva to convince Petra. Rita thinks Uncle Corry's a weird guy. She said, "We can't do that to the woman."

I told her that Uncle Corry was pretty nice and not so weird at all, but then I had to name all of his good qualities so she could make a little list. "He likes fishing," I said.

She didn't think that was a good quality. She didn't write it down.

"He likes eating well," I said.

She didn't think that was a good quality either.

I said it *was* a good quality because what if one of them likes eating well and the other doesn't, then it doesn't make any sense to cook well. Eating is really important.

"Well, okay," said Rita. She wrote it down.

"He likes to watch television," I said.

She didn't think *that* was a good quality either.

I said it was a good quality because watching television together is fun. What if one likes it and the other doesn't, how do things go from there? But she didn't want to put it down on the list.

"He likes drinking beer," I said. "He goes to the café every Friday night and sometimes on other nights too."

"Okay, stop right there," said Rita. "You're only naming stupid or boring qualities. Name something good, or else I'm out."

"He's pretty nice," I said. "He takes care of his family when his family has problems."

"So, is he taking care of you?" Rita asked. "If you ask me, you're taking care of him, not the other way around. You cook, he does nothing."

"He's calm. That's a good quality too."

Luckily she wrote that down.

"He can tell good stories." I was thinking of the brown bean story. "He tells stories about all kinds of things."

She wrote this down too. Now I was coming into my stride. I told her about a whole lot of good qualities:

— He reads a lot (just *Angling and Anglers*, but I didn't say that).

— He can talk and listen well (lately at least he's not *not* talking and *not* listening the whole time).

— He's really interested in sports (fishing is a sport too).

— He's generous (cookie-tin money).

— He has a sense of humor (a not-cool sense of humor, but at least he laughs now and then).

— He's very popular and has a lot of friends (at the café—I've never seen any of them, but I didn't say that).

— He likes being with people (or else he wouldn't go to the café).

Now we had a whole list.

"Good," said Rita. "But you'll have to make sure he does something about his appearance. He really looks terrible. She'll run away screaming if she sees him like that."

Rita phoned the list through to Eva and then Eva called Petra. So at first Petra didn't want to give it a try, but later she decided she did. "Well, okay," said Rita—that's what Eva said Petra had said—"but if it's no fun, I'll be out of there in five minutes." So now she's going down to The WunderBar, the café where Uncle Corry always is, on Friday night.

I'm hatching a plan to get him to go to the barber and have him buy some new clothes. It would be a lot easier if a blind date did mean that you kept your eyes shut or covered your eyes with a jacket on the date.

evening:
Ate rotini (or whatever they're called, those screw-shaped things).

I said, "Shouldn't you go to the barber sometime?"

"Why?" he asked.

"And buy some new clothes?"

"Why?"

"Like, you know, just to do it. It's cool."

"What do you mean? Is there maybe something wrong with the way I look?"

Now it was getting dangerous. Of course, I couldn't say yes because maybe he'd get angry and the whole plan would fall through. He needed to be in a good mood for the plan to work. On the other hand, I couldn't say no because then he'd think he looked good and he wouldn't change anything. I had to come up with something between yes and no, but I couldn't find a word between yes and no. So, I said, "Uh … yes and no. Something in between."

"What do you mean, 'yes and no, something in between'?"

"It could be better," I said. "It's not bad, but it's not everything. It's … a kind of 6 on a scale of 10."

"A 6?"

"A 6 minus. That's what you get at school if you didn't do a totally bad job but not a really good one either. Wouldn't you prefer to be a 10?"

Uncle Corry had just stuffed his mouth full of rotini. There was a dribble of sauce on his chin. He stopped chewing and stared at me.

"Wha? Uh hen?"

"Yes, a 10," I said. (I've become pretty expert in the meantime at understanding Uncle Corry with his mouth full.)

"Hy?" He started chewing again. I waited until he had swallowed.

"Girls like 10s more. They find 10s cooler than 6 minuses."

"'Girls'? What do you mean, 'girls'? What are you talking about?"

"Like, you know, women, whatever. A 6 minus is pretty okay, but only a 10 makes them really happy. Then they jump up and down and cheer, they're so happy."

He put his spoon down. (Uncle Corry eats everything with a spoon, not a fork. He thinks forks are clumsy.) "What do you mean exactly?" he asked. His eyes narrowed.

I was feeling more and more uneasy. If only I'd never started. It was a rotten plan. It would never work. What was I getting into anyway? What difference did it make to me if he had a wife or not, if he ate well or not? What did that have to do with me? It was none of my business, but I couldn't back down now.

"Uh, well, it's like this … I was thinking, maybe you'd like to have a wife, or a girlfriend—somebody who'll cook for you and stuff. That'd be nice. Wouldn't it?"

"And?" His eyes were still narrowed. He fixed them on me. I had to come up with a rock-solid story. That much was clear.

"Well, you're always alone," I said. "Not now, because I'm here. But otherwise you would be. Wouldn't you like that—having a wife? Or a girlfriend?"

It was quiet for a moment. His eyes slowly returned to normal.

He looked at his plate. "Uh … well, I don't know. It *is* nice and quiet the way it is. Women are always nagging you to death."

"Not all of them," I said. "There are women who don't nag you to death, too. I know lots of them."

"So, who?"

"Petra, for example. She never whines and she's really nice."

"Petra? Who's Petra?"

"Petra is a woman."

"Yeah, I got that far too. What do you mean 'Petra'? Where'd you get that idea?"

"She'd like to meet you."

Uncle Corry grabbed the table to steady himself. That was sensible, I think, because you could tell from his face that otherwise he'd have tumbled over for sure, chair and all. "Come again? What? So who is she anyway? And how … what?"

"She's pretty nice looking. Nice hair, nice clothes. So, I thought maybe your hair could be a little nicer and your clothes too. I'm sure she'd like that."

"But how …? Huh? And what …?"

"She's coming down to the café Friday night. So, you've still got enough time for the barber and stuff."

"Friday? Excuse me?"

My plate was empty. It seemed like a good idea to be gone for a little while. "I'm going over to Rita's," I said and got up.

"Come back!" I could hear him shout. "What's the story with …?"

I swung the front door shut behind me.

When I came home, I tried to sneak through the hallway to my room, but the living-room door flew open and he grabbed me by the collar. "No way," he said. "I have no idea what all you've been cooking up, but no way. You just better make sure she stays away. Are you completely out of your gourd?!"

Crap. Now I have to call Rita tomorrow to tell her she has to call Eva to tell her she has to call Petra to tell her it's off.

I don't understand why Corry makes things so difficult—instead of being happy that I've arranged something for him! He does nothing on his own. I've had enough. I'm never going to do anything anymore. Everybody can deal with it all themselves.

Thursday, August 4

10:30 in the morning:

It's on! It worked!

We're going downtown in a minute (barber, clothes!). He doesn't want to go by himself. I have to go with him.

Just gave Rita a quick call so she can call Eva so she can call Petra to say that it'll be at another café tomorrow.

evening:

So, miracles do happen—the kinds of things you know for sure are impossible that turn out to be possible after all. Now I've finally even seen a couple of them, with my own eyes no less.

Uncle Corry Looks Good! Well, better, at any rate. I don't think Petra will run away screaming if she sees him like this.

First we went to the barber. Uncle Corry whined nonstop and warned the barber every other minute that it would not be a good thing if he ended up looking ridiculous. Finally the barber was so fed up that he said, "Now, listen here, more ridiculous than when you walked in is impossible. So just zip it for a minute, please. It's driving me crazy. I can't work like this!" He held the scissors threateningly close to Corry's face.

I cringed. I knew for sure that Uncle Corry would get furious and storm out of the place with his hair half-cut (leaving me behind with no money to pay the bill), but that didn't happen. He sat there and even stopped whining. "All right, then," he said. "Just do it the way you think it should be" (first miracle).

It did take me some getting used to when it was done. His

hair is totally different now. Nicer, but it is *totally* different. Uncle Corry himself was satisfied though (second miracle). The barber looked relieved.

It seems to me it would be pretty hard being a barber. You have to keep everybody happy and you get all kinds of different people under your scissors. I don't think I would dare do it. If you cut wrong by accident, that's not a good thing—you'll definitely be crucified.

We walked around downtown and went into a men's store.

"Can I help you?" a man asked us.

Uncle Corry looked warily around the store.

"What are you looking for?" the men's clothing salesman asked.

"Clothes," I replied.

"Really?" The men's clothing salesman looked very surprised. "I thought perhaps you were here for flowers or cigarettes."

"We don't smoke," I said. "It makes your clothes stink." I pointed at Uncle Corry, who was already pulling trousers off a shelf. "He needs clothes for a date, a blind date."

"Aha!" said the man. "A blind date. Daygajay or formal?" (I don't know exactly how you write "*daygajay.*" I'm sure it's not like that, but that's the way you pronounce it, so I'll just write it like that.)

"Uncle Corry," I called. He was now standing even further away, looking at the price tag on a shirt. "Daygajay or formal?"

"What?" he called back.

"The blind date! Is it daygajay or formal? I don't know what that means, 'daygajay.'"

In two seconds, Corry was standing beside us. "Shut your trap," he whispered loudly. "Everybody doesn't have to know!"

"*Daygajay* is, let's say, leisure clothing," said the man. "Relaxed clothing, but well groomed and stylish. Not a jogging suit, obviously." He smiled.

"Then let's do daygajay," I said. Relaxed clothing seemed appropriate for Uncle Corry. He was acting pretty stressed out.

To make a long story short (I don't have a new journal yet), the third miracle took place in this store. We must have been there two hours, and the clothing man was starting to look pretty desperate after the first hour (Uncle Corry had something to say about a lot of the clothes), but it worked. Uncle Corry was all newly decked out. He had:

— A new pair of trousers (a light color, very appropriate for the summer, the man said, but could certainly still be worn in the fall)

— A new shirt (white) (This really did look good on him!)

— A new jacket (blue) (It was on the edge of daygajay, said the man. The jacket bore a hint of formal in it, and this gave a subtle and stylish touch to the whole look)

— New socks (blue with thin stripes).

The socks caused some problems though. Corry didn't want to buy them. He thought it a crime to milk people for so much money for something as trivial as socks. He could get them for €1.29 a pair at the store down the street where he always bought his socks and underwear. However, the clothing man said that, on the contrary, socks were very important for the total look and that's where the subtle difference lay between taste and lack of taste.

"Nobody'll see," said Uncle Corry. "They're in my shoes and under my pants."

"That's what you think," said the man. "When you sit down, your trousers pull up, and then you see them. These kinds of details show true taste. There are hordes of women who will lose interest in a man on account of the wrong socks. Or are you planning to have your girlfriend stand all night?"

Uncle Corry had no answer to that. I did. I would have said, But she's not going to look under the table, is she? But I didn't. It seemed wiser not to. The man did know a lot about clothing other than that.

It was a tasteful ensemble, said the clothing man when Uncle Corry had everything on at the same time. I could hardly believe my eyes when he came out of the dressing room with everything on at the same time. He was just about unrecognizable now, with his new hair *and* new clothes.

Uncle Corry almost couldn't believe his eyes when he saw the bill, although he grumbled for only a few seconds. (Too long, as far as the man was concerned, I believe. He made a funny face when Uncle Corry said he'd never yet seen anything like it. "Nor have I," he replied as he looked up, like he was hoping for last-minute help from God.)

"The outfit needs new shoes to go with it," I said as we walked out of the store. I looked at his feet. "Those old sneakers don't really fit with the rest. It's no longer a tasteful ensemble that way."

"Jeez! I haven't even had a single date yet and already it's cost me an arm and a leg, bled me dry. I'm handing over a year's income to those frigging stores!"

"You will have a stylish *look* though," I said.

Uncle Corry went into the absolutely cheapest shoe store he could find, in search of the absolutely cheapest shoes that fit with the look. He found them (on my advice). They were still too expensive for him, but he did buy them, grumbling. "Women. Always the same story. You always have to be different than you are. They always want to change you. Just look, I haven't even had a single date and I already have to totally change."

Suddenly I couldn't take it anymore. "Oh, just stop your whining," I said. "You say that women whine, but if anybody's whining, it's you." I surprised myself, saying it to him like that, but I meant it. So, this must be the right way to tackle Uncle Corry. The barber did it, I did it, and it worked. He stopped whining.

I think it's pretty complicated, clothes and all that. Seems like you have to take all kinds of things into account. That man in the store was pretty nice and really helpful (especially the first half hour). He told me all kinds of things about clothes, about what did and didn't fit together and why. I tried to remember it all, but I can't recall the half of it anymore.

Just looked at the socks in my closet. I'm worried. Aren't they the wrong socks? How do you know what's wrong?

Just quickly about this morning, when I still thought it wasn't going to happen. (I haven't written about that yet.)

I went over to the phone. I said, "I'm going to call Rita so she can call Eva to tell her to call Petra to tell her it's off."

"Wait a minute," said Uncle Corry.

I waited.

"I've been thinking. Maybe it's not such a terrible idea. I don't know."

"It's a good idea," I said.

"I don't know," he said.

"Then I won't call," I said.

"Good," he said.

Shortly after that I had to call anyway. He didn't want her to come to his café. That's where all his buddies were, he said. The two of them wouldn't be left alone, and he'd be hearing about it for years. "Just say she should go to The Cherry at eight thirty."

"They're good clothes," said Uncle Corry tonight at dinner. "And my hair … You were … well, like, I'm … you know."

"You look good," I said. "I don't think she'll run away screaming."

I meant it.

Got new cooking pay. I only had to ask for it once.

Friday, August 5

Uncle Corry's driving me crazy. He's pacing around the house all the time.

"Just go sit down somewhere and relax," I said. I got him a little stack of *Angling and Anglers*. He sat down, but after ten seconds he was already up again.

I hope I don't start acting that weird someday, sometime when I have a date. I'm sure I won't. Act weird, I mean, not that I won't have a date. I don't understand why he's acting so nervous. I'm always setting things up with people, like with Rita, but then I don't go and act like a retard, do I?

evening:
"You know what?" Corry said this afternoon all of a sudden. "We're going to fix up your room."

"I can't," I said. "I already arranged to see Rita."

"You see her every day. You can stay here just once, can't you?"

"We'll need paint," I said. "And then tonight you'll be covered with splotches of paint and have paint spatters in your hair."

He hadn't thought of that. "Then we'll go clean up the magazines," he said.

So we did. It's really empty in here now. It was a whole production, though, by the way—especially finding a spot to put them. We looked in Corry's closets. They're all totally bursting with old clothes and other junk.

"Why don't you throw some stuff away?" I asked.

"Like what?" he asked.

"Well, like this." I held up an ugly pair of plaid pants. "They smell like you last had them on in the Middle Ages."

"You crazy?" he exclaimed. "Those are good trousers. I've had them for fifteen years and they're still not worn."

It's all in what you call not worn. Fifteen years! Those pants are older than I am. They belong in a museum.

"But when do you wear them?" I asked. "I've never seen you in them yet."

"Well, sometimes. Not that often. In fact never. But I'm going to."

"So, when? When was the last time you wore them?"

"Uh … well, about ten years ago, I think. I'm not getting rid of them!"

So that's the way it went with everything. After an hour or two, there still wasn't any room in the closet. He only got rid of a couple of old pairs of underwear (while objecting), ones he didn't even know he had. There were holes in them and the elastic in the waistbands had gotten all hard. They made a crackling sound, and if you moved them back and forth a little they broke right away.

The good thing, though, was that we were two hours further along without him pacing around.

Then the phone rang. Rita. Where was I?

"We're cleaning Corry's closets," I said.

"We were supposed to get together," she said.

I looked at the clock. It was three o'clock already, even though I was supposed to be at her place around two.

"He's pretty nervous," I said, "about tonight."

"So what? That doesn't mean you have to go and clean his closets for him."

"That way he has something to do and he's not thinking about it all the time."

"He can effing clean by himself!"

I didn't know what to do. I wanted to go to Rita's, but I didn't like leaving Corry alone. Crap. Everybody wants something from me all the time. I have to be everywhere at the same time. How am I supposed to be everywhere at the same time?

I said I'd be there in a few minutes. Uncle Corry didn't like the fact that I was going, but I went anyway.

Rita and I talked about the movie. She has ideas. She also wants a lot of music in the movie, music that her mother liked.

"So, what did she like?" I asked.

"I don't know," she said. "I still have to ask. But I do know she liked music."

I said it was a good idea but that you do end up with all that old music in your movie. It'll be one of those old-fashioned movies, then.

"So what?"

"Like, well, okay."

Rita had even come up with a couple of questions we can ask the family members:

— What's your favorite memory of Anneke?

— Was she a good student at school?

— Was she good at sports?

If you ask me, there are better questions than that, but I didn't say so because then I'd have to think them up and I don't know anything about her yet.

Tomorrow night we're going to see Gea. She's the first of Rita's mom's sisters we're going to interview.

—

Uncle Corry's finally gone, although it was a huge hassle. I had cooked rice. It was really delicious (it's called paella, a Spanish dish, according to *Tasty & Healthy*), but he ate almost nothing. He said it was because of the date that he wasn't hungry. I hope he doesn't keep that up. The plan was made specifically so he would get a girlfriend who'd be able to cook for him once I'm gone. Although, if he loses his appetite over a girlfriend, he might as well *not* have a girlfriend because it won't matter if she cooks for him or not.

I had given him a really good description of what Petra looks like, but he must have asked at least fifty times, "How am I going to recognize her? How do I know it's her? When I get there, I won't recognize her."

"Then she'll recognize you," I said. I had given Rita a description of the new Corry and she had passed it on to Eva, who in turn passed it on to Petra. It came in handy that I knew exactly what he was going to wear. I could even describe his socks. Rita thought that was nonsense, though, the sock description. "You think she's going to look under the pants of all the men who come in there to see what kind of socks they're wearing?"

"When somebody sits down, though, you *do* see what kind of socks he's wearing," I said. "Socks are very important."

"Socks are totally unimportant," said Rita, and with that the subject was closed as far as she was concerned. I tried to keep on about it, but she just interrupted me by talking about something else. Rita obviously has no sense for these things—not for style, not for taste.

—

I'm a little bored. I don't feel like watching TV. I don't feel like writing anymore. Maybe I'll just go clean the closets. Half of all the stacks of *Angling and Anglers* have now been stuffed into the closets and half are still in Corry's bedroom on the floor. If Petra should ever come spend the night sometime, she might trip over them. I'm sure she wouldn't like that.

nighttime (2:20 a.m.):
Corry's back. The front door woke me up. It slammed shut pretty loudly. He's drunk. He'd gone to The WunderBar after the date. I'm pretty pissed off. I stayed up all that time just to hear how it went, until I just about collapsed. Instead of him taking that into account and coming home, he just calmly went to the café to drink beer (a whole lot).

He said he'd made a stupid mistake by going over there. He had clean forgotten that he looked totally different than usual, with his new hair and new clothes. His friends at the café had asked if he'd been out romancing.

"So what if I was?" Uncle Corry had said.

They had all just about fallen off their barstools, laughing. They had all made sick jokes. "Must've been with a woman from the loony bin," said one. "Who else would want a date with Corry?"

"No, no, no!" cried another. "Not with a woman. With a *fag!* Juz look at that getup!"

"With a loony-bin fag!" a third person had shouted. Everybody (except for Corry) had a grand old time. Even Kurt, the bar owner, had chimed in.

"But how did things go with Petra?" I asked.

"I said, 'Nothing but a bunch of jerks. Just keep right on sitting there at the bar with all your pathetic bull, for all I care. You're full of crap.'"

"But how did the date go?"

"Bunch of over-aged losers. Blowhard scum. They just sit there. Shit on everything and everybody. But do something themselves? Whoa."

"But was it fun? What did she say? What did you say?"

"Get themselves loaded. *That* they can do. Full of crap. Full of stinking crap. I've had it up to here with them."

"I'm going to bed," I said. "If you're not going to say anything, I'm going back to sleep."

"Vermin's what they are. The whole stinking lot of them. Somebody should grab them and shove their faces in shit."

"I'm going."

"They should send the extermins ... the ... those pest whatzits after them."

I left. You can't get a normal word out of Corry when he's been drinking. I do hate that. Work your butt off for somebody and what do you get in return? Nothing, just drunken babble about excrement. Ugh.

Saturday, August 6

It's not going to work out between him and that Petra woman, said Corry. I asked how he could know that so soon, after only one date.

"She said so. She said, 'It's not going to work out between us.'"

"Oh."

"I was a nice guy, she said. Honestly very nice and so on. But it wasn't going to turn into anything."

"Why not?"

"We didn't fit with each other, she said."

"Oh." I wondered how you could know so quickly whether you fit with somebody.

"She thought it was a fun evening, she said. It was. A lot of fun. We talked. From eight thirty to almost eleven."

I didn't really know what I was supposed to say. I felt a little guilty. It was because of me that he had bought all those new clothes, and now it wasn't going to turn into anything. "Too bad about the new clothes," I said to say something.

Uncle Corry stared off, frowning. "No," he said. "I'm glad."

"That it's not going to work out?"

"No, that I tried. It's also a good thing that I went to the bar last night."

"Huh? Why?" Hadn't he had a rotten time?

"A bunch of pathetic jerks. And I'm one of them, one of the barflies, the stool fossils. I don't want that. I want something else."

"Like what?"

"I don't know yet."

"Maybe you should talk with Tineke," I said. "She knows a lot."

"Tineke? Who's Tineke?"

"Tineke. She was here not too long ago. She brought me to the doctor's. You didn't want her in the house."

"Oh, her."

"Yes, her."

"I'll see."

I'm going to run downtown in a minute to buy videotape for the interview with Gea tonight. We haven't gotten money from any of the family members yet, but I'll advance it.

Sunday, August 7

She's gone now. I feel really weird—kind of full and empty at the same time, like I have to cry even though there aren't any tears. The tears have run dry without being cried. I don't even know where to begin with writing everything down. Then again, I don't feel like writing everything down. It's like I have to though. Something or somebody's making me—like something bad will happen if I don't.

I heard the doorbell and Corry's voice, too, but not hers. Suddenly she was standing in my room while I was lying on my bed, writing.

"Hi there, Maurits." She's the only one who always calls me Maurits.

Everybody is mad at me because I didn't show up: Rita—because we were supposed to go see Gea for the interview, and all the Geeks—because I was supposed to film their gig.

Rita called to find out what was keeping me. She didn't even let me finish what I was saying. I said, "Sorry, I can't make it tonight, my m—"

"Well, then don't come," she snapped. "I'll just do it by myself. I've been waiting for you this whole time, like I did yesterday too. You didn't show up then either—without saying anything. I have better things to do. I've had it. Screw you!" She slammed the receiver down.

After that, Danny called. He was mad too. "What gives?" he shouted. "We should have been playing already." Only then did

I remember that I was supposed to film them playing Saturday night. (I had clean forgotten because of all the hassle with Uncle Corry the past few days.)

I explained what was going on. He let me finish talking, but it didn't make much of a difference. He stayed mad anyway. "This is the stupidest, lamest, rotten little excuse I've ever heard! Can't you come up with anything better?"

"It's the truth!"

"What kind of a sorry douche are you?! You've got an important job, dude! And you don't show up because your mommy's visiting? You better get over here. Now!"

"I'm not coming. I really can't. Sorry, I—"

Buzzzzz. He had slammed down the receiver.

So, I guess that's the way it goes. You work your butt off to get friends and work, you make one little mistake, and all those friends and work are gone just like that.

Maybe none of it matters though. I'm sure I don't have to stay here that long anymore. The doctor told my mom she could easily go home for a weekend because she was already doing a lot better.

I'd have liked it better if she really had gone home and called me to come, but she said that wasn't such a good idea. It was better for her not go to "that house," as she put it, just yet. Maybe she would get confused again since everything would get stirred up and resurface. And it was better for me too. I was used to things here by now. All that back-and-forth business wasn't good for a kid. "Kids need stability," she said.

We cooked together. She thought I did an awesome job. She was proud of me, she said, not just because of the cooking but because of everything. I was doing everything really well.

"How so, everything?" I asked.

"Well, you know, everything. Isn't that true?" She called for Corry to come join us. "Don't you agree that Maurits is doing fabulously?"

"Doing what?" asked Corry.

"Well, you know, everything," she said.

"He's a pretty good guy," said Corry. "Nothing wrong with him."

She ran her fingers through my hair. "My little man," she said.

I don't know. I thought she was acting a little over the top, not crazy or anything, but ... well, I don't know. I hope it's not contagious over there. I'm sure there are a lot of weird people running around there who *are* crazy. My mom's not (of course). She's around it all day long, though, so maybe you get a little weird yourself. In fact, she makes little jokes about it all the time. "At our nuthouse ...," she'll say, or "At my institution ..." I don't like that, because then she acts like she's crazy, too, and that's not true. For example, when she started to cook the green beans, she said, "At our nuthouse, they cook all the vegetables for as long as it takes till they're almost mush. That way, the crazies with false teeth that don't fit well can get their greens down too. Ha, ha, ha! And there are a lot of them, crazies with false teeth. They could start a chatterbox orchestra: clackety-clack, clackety-clack-clack-clack—all keeping time." She chattered her own (real!) teeth up and down a couple of times.

"Don't act so stupid," I snapped. It was all bad enough already. I really wasn't in the mood for jokes like that. Why didn't she act normal?

"What's wrong?" she asked. "Aren't you happy I'm here?"

"Sure," I said. "Of course I am." I was, but I felt a little ... I don't know what it's called. She came so unexpectedly. I don't understand why she didn't just call ahead of time. That way I could already have been getting used to the idea. Everything suddenly felt different. The whole house felt different. I felt different too. Corry felt different. Everything.

That night I asked her—why she hadn't called, I mean.

"It was a surprise," she said. "Don't you think it was a nice surprise?"

"Sure. Of course I do. But—"

"But?"

"But ... I don't know. It was so sudden. At least I would have known."

"But I'm your mother! I assume you always like seeing me. I always like seeing you. Don't you like seeing me?"

"Sure, of course I do."

"So?! If you don't like it, you can go right ahead and say so, you know, and I'll leave."

"No, I think it's nice you're here. Honest."

"Well, okay then."

And again she told me that things were a lot better, the worst was over, but it all still needed some time. Of course, an awful lot had happened lately—and before that too. A lot was coming out, other things too, things from long ago that she had never really looked at that way before. The doctors there were really helping her get a better perspective on things. None of it was easy, she said. It was hard.

"So, what kinds of things are you getting a better perspective on?"

"A lot of things. From long ago too." She looked at Corry. "Maybe you should talk about it, too, sometime. We went through a lot at home long ago."

"Like what?" Corry asked.

"Well, all kinds of things. With Daddy and Ma and so on, and how they were. That Daddy died so young and that Ma later—"

"That's all history. It happened. That's it."

My mom sighed. "Yes. Well. In any case, we talk a lot about that too. And of course, we talk about …" She shook her head. "Let's keep things light," she said. "I don't feel like … I'm here now. So, what are you up to, Maurits? Are things a little to your liking?"

I really wanted to tell her I'd gotten a card from my dad, from Memphis, U.S.A., but it didn't seem wise to start talking about him. I tried to come up with something else to talk about, but just when I'd found something and wanted to start talking about the movie about Rita's mom and my awesome sponsor plan, the phone rang and I had that conversation with Rita.

"Who was that?" my mom asked when I'd hung up.

"Rita," I said. "I was supposed to meet with her, but I forgot all about it because you were suddenly here."

"Well, you can always see her. Rita. Is that your girlfriend?"

I had told her about Rita over the phone before, but she had obviously forgotten. "Not my girlfriend, just a friend. At least she was. Not anymore. She's mad."

"She'll come around again, Maurits. Don't worry. Gee, Corry, nice to see you again. It's been a long time, hasn't it? You look good. You do, I really think so. Things are obviously going well for you. I can see that."

Corry had his new pants and shirt on again. He mumbled

something along the lines of "not so bad." After that he said he'd just gone to the barber.

"The barber!" she exclaimed. "Remember how Ma used to always insist on cutting our hair herself? That saved money."

"You always cut my hair too," I said.

"But I do it nicely," she said. (Huh? It's all in what you think is nice! I've walked around like an idiot often enough.) "Our mother," she went on, "so your grandma, always cut off a bunch. Then she'd see it was crooked, so she'd cut off another chunk to straighten it out. Then the other side would be crooked, and so on until you almost had no hair left on your head. Remember that, Corry?"

"Yeah," said Corry. "I remember."

"Gee, Corry, that you're still living here. How long have you been living here already? If I'm not mistaken, at least twenty years or so, isn't that right? Aren't you ever in the mood for something different? Something bigger?"

"It agrees with me here. Low rent, nice neighborhood."

"Hmm."

"Hmm?"

"Well, if you think it's a nice neighborhood … I'd never want to live here again. What do you think of it, Maurits?"

"It's okay. Do you mean you lived here too?"

"Yes, we grew up nearby, a couple of streets farther down. Is the house still there, Corry?"

"No. They tore down the whole business over there. Neighborhood renewal."

They talked about the neighborhood for a while and who was still here and who no longer lived here, and then the phone rang again, which was Danny calling.

"Who was that?" my mom asked.

"Danny," I said. "From The Geeks. I was supposed to film them tonight, but I forgot."

"The Geeks?"

"That's a band, a really good one. I was going to film them playing tonight. Now they're mad."

"They'll come around again. Don't worry."

I couldn't get to sleep last night. When I finally did, I had all kinds of scary dreams. Most of them I forgot. I still remember, though, that suddenly all my teeth fell out of my mouth and that I needed false teeth. Off and on I kept waking up, too, and then I wouldn't know where I was for a second.

My mom slept on the couch in the living room. I asked if she wouldn't prefer to sleep in my bed and I'd sleep on the couch, but that wasn't necessary, she said. I could just sleep in my own bed. What did she mean, my own bed? My own bed's at home. I didn't like her saying that. She acted just like I *live* here instead of like I'm staying here.

Hey, maybe *that's* it, the reason everything felt so weird the whole time. I'm here and my mom's coming over to visit me. She's a guest, even though I'm a guest as well. That's not what it felt like though. It's just like I'm living here with Corry and like she's just coming over for a little visit. It feels strange. *She* seemed strange, like I don't really know her, but then again like I do—like a stranger and a familiar person at the same time.

I felt kind of alone, really, more alone than before when she wasn't here. I don't really get any of this.

—

So, she's gone now. Corry is ordering pizzas tonight. "I'm sure you don't feel like cooking," he said.

"No, not much."

"Me neither," he said. (Like he *ever* cooks!)

I was allowed to choose what I felt like eating: french fries, Chinese takeout, or pizza. I chose pizza (I don't dare eat Chinese anymore since that dog story) (even though I don't believe a word of it).

"I don't understand why she didn't just call ahead of time," I told him. "Suddenly she was just here."

"Typical. She doesn't think. I'd have liked to have known too. I would have cleaned this dump up a bit, arranged for a mattress. But that's the way she is. Typical."

"It sounds like you don't think she's very nice," I said.

It was quiet for a moment. "Sure I do," he said. "She's my sister. But we're very different. I'm easygoing, she's more … well, difficult. And she's got these tendencies. She never takes other people into account."

"Takes me into account," I said.

"Yeah," said Corry. "You, she does. So, pizza it is?"

I'm going to stop writing for now. Tomorrow, buy a new journal.

Hey! I'm suddenly thinking I don't feel as bad as I did this afternoon when I started writing. My headache's almost gone too.

Monday, August 8

There was a difficult moment when she left yesterday afternoon. She cried and didn't even try not to. She hugged me and just about crushed me. She said she missed me so much and that she hoped everything would be all right again soon and that we'd be together soon and a lot more. I felt a weird rock in my throat, but I didn't have to cry. And now comes the very worst part:

No, I'm not going to write it down. It's too awful. I just don't get it either. Well, okay, I'll write it really small, so small that I can't even read it:

I was really kind of relieved when she was gone.

Only a little, but still. I didn't get it, because she is my mom. I got a really bad headache right away. (It felt just like sagging brain, but even worse, worse than ever before.) I felt guilty and rotten and a whole bunch else all at the same time.

It sounds really bad, but it's just like she ruined something or whatever by coming here, but I don't know exactly *what*, even though I was really glad to see her—honest—really glad.

When she was gone, Corry and I flopped down on the couch. We sat there a long time without saying anything.

"So, that was your mother," said Corry.

"Yeah, that was my mother," I said.

"She's gone now."

"She's gone."

And then I suddenly felt that, what I wrote in small letters, I mean. It scared me. I hadn't expected it.

I called Tineke. I can go see her this afternoon.

First, I'm going to buy a journal. Then I'll go see her.

evening:
Tineke said I didn't need to be scared that I didn't love my mother anymore or that I loved her any less. So, I asked her what *was* the reason I felt that way. She didn't really know. "But I think it's because you've been through a whole lot too," she said. "And your mother wasn't there when you were going through it. Meanwhile, you've built up a whole new life here in a short period of time. Alone, without her. You have to get used to her again, I think. And on top of that, she really threw you for a loop by suddenly showing up like that. Didn't she?"

Yes. But still.

She also said that I should see Rita really soon and Rita was sure not to stay mad for long. I would just have to explain it. She was sure she'd understand. And Danny ... well, I could call Danny, too, if I really wanted to, although she understood that it would be hard to explain. He didn't know anything about the circumstances. For most people it's nothing special for their mothers to come over. For me it is, because of the whole situation—but of course The Geeks wouldn't know that.

I don't really dare go over to Rita's. What if she's *still* mad? She can be so intense sometimes. I don't know yet. I'm going to wait a little while on that.

nighttime (± 2:00 a.m.):
I didn't like cooking with her either. She didn't know where anything was, and she was really clumsy, even though she kept acting like *she* was cooking and I was just helping her out a little. "This has

to go in here, Maurits, not in *there*." "No, Maurits, you shouldn't cut it like *that*. Just let me do it." "No, it needs more salt"—and so on.

I even told her, "Why don't you just sit down and I'll cook."

"I wouldn't hear of it," she said. "I'm your mother. I'll cook for you."

"But we're in Corry's house," I said. "It's *his* kitchen."

"So what?"

"I'm used to cooking here. I do it all the time."

So, that's when she said she thought I was doing it all so well, everything and stuff.

later (± 5:17 a.m.):

She brought me breakfast in bed in the morning and sat down beside me.

"What an uncomfortable room," she said.

"We're going to fix it up," I said. "We already started."

"I don't understand how Corry can live here." Her eyes wandered down to the wall behind me where my father's postcards are hung up. I hoped she would say something about them, but she didn't.

"What's going to happen when school starts again?" I asked. "Am I supposed to go to school here?"

"Let's not think about that yet," she said.

"But it's not a long way off anymore."

"I'm sure I'll be back by then," she said.

"But if you're not?"

"I don't know." She suddenly sounded a little irritated. "I just don't know. We'll see."

I wanted to ask what would happen if my dad was already back by then, before she was, but I didn't dare. I was hoping she would say something about that herself, but she didn't.

"Everything will be all right, Maurits," she said. "Believe me. Everything will be all right. It's a little hard right now, but it will be all right."

I really wanted to believe her. I tried my best to believe her, but there was something, I don't know what, something that made it so I couldn't.

In a minute I'm going to try and sleep again. I keep thinking about the weekend, about everything she said and did, over and over again, like I'm looking for an answer to something I don't even know the question to. I wish you could just turn off your thoughts. I keep trying to think of something else, but then I start thinking about Rita and I start getting (uncomfortably) warm all over because my thoughts keep ending up at how angry she was and that I have to go see her to make things right again. So then I start thinking about my mom again. Now I'm going to try to think about something totally different—about a cool dog, like, a dog I can take for walks and go swimming with.

7: 10 a.m.:
Just had a really weird dream. There was a really strong wind, a kind of whirlwind, and it sucked everything up in the air. A whole flock of sheep hung there like some huge white sheep cloud. Then geese came and they died. It wasn't really a nightmare, but it wasn't much fun either, about the geese, I mean. The sheep were okay, even though I was worried that they'd all fall down dead soon. Steven was there too.

I wouldn't mind seeing Steven. He'll be going back to school again soon and I might not be there. I guess they're still at their cottage in France. I would have liked to have gone with them—this summer would have been very different—but, looking back, I'm glad I couldn't go. The two weeks I spent with them before summer vacation started were okay, but all the arguments made me feel really weird. Steven's brothers and sister bugged each other, acted like jerks, and were loud all day (Steven too).

Actually those two weeks weren't okay at all. They were terrible. I tried to be invisible the whole time so I wouldn't bother anybody. They were all stressed out. I got the feeling that things in that house were way too busy already and that I was only making it worse. So somewhere it was a big relief that I didn't fit in the car (even though I didn't like having to go to Uncle Corry's, since I didn't know him at all).

I don't think it's so bad that I'm here. Yes, I'd obviously rather be home, although I think I won't go live at home on my own. I mean, I'd rather be at home, but everything would have to be normal again, and everything's not normal. I don't see how everything could become normal again in a hurry either.

11:45 in the morning (so, Tuesday, August 9):
I just woke up! I can't understand how I slept so long. I didn't at all mean to go back to sleep!

Tuesday, August 9

I didn't like the fact that she didn't say one word about my dad all weekend either. Doesn't he exist or something?

She wanted to cut my hair. "It's getting much too long," she said.

"No," I said. "I like long hair. I want to keep it this way."

"What's gotten into you, Maurits?" she said. "Just let me cut it. Corry, do you have a pair of scissors?"

"No," I said. "I don't want a haircut."

"He doesn't want one," said Corry.

"Don't you get involved," said my mom.

"You didn't want your mother to cut your hair when you were little either," I said. "Why do I have to put up with it?"

"My mother couldn't cut hair."

You can't either was on the tip of my tongue, but I didn't say it.

"Just leave the boy alone," said Corry.

My mom looked at Corry, then at me, and then at Corry again. After that, she sat down on the couch with a hurt look in her eyes. She didn't say anything.

This afternoon, Corry suddenly said, "That guy gave me a good haircut, didn't he?"

"He certainly did," I said. "A really good one."

"Did you know that's the first time in my life I ever went to a barber?"

"Really?"

"I always cut my own hair."

"Really?"

"But the barber does do a better job."

"Yeah."

"If you want to go to the barber, all you have to do is ask. I'll pay for it."

"Oh."

"I didn't want to say anything to your mother, but she looked just like Ma, your grandma, I mean, when she wanted to cut your hair and you didn't want her to. I was thinking, Don't say anything 'cause she'll hit the ceiling. She doesn't want to be like Ma, but she is like Ma."

"Really?"

"Yeah. And then right away I thought, I'll just give Rits some money if he wants to go to the barber, but I didn't want to say that while she was around. You don't have to have your hair cut by your mother if you don't want, don't you think? Jesus, she really made me think of Ma. She could go on and on about that kind of thing, too, but I decided not to say that."

I've discovered more about my family these past couple of weeks than in all the past thirteen years put together.

To the barber tomorrow.

later:

I went over to Rita's. It had to happen sometime. She wasn't mad at all. I wish I'd gone sooner. As it is, I got all worked up over nothing.

I explained that my mother had come by unexpectedly.

"Oh," she said. "Why didn't you say so?"

That's a good one!

"You hung up on me," I said.

"Oh, well, I was pissed off," she said. "That happens."

"Not anymore?" I asked.

"Of course not. I was thinking I'm sure he's got something important going on. I just thought it was dumb that you didn't call."

"I didn't think to call," I said. "That was because, I was—"

"Okay, enough of that. Let's not go on about it."

She's going to the barber's with me tomorrow.

Wednesday morning, August 10

Last night I finally slept normally again. This morning I lay in bed thinking that I'm still really glad she came. My mom, I mean. All of a sudden I don't even really understand why I was making such a big deal about it. I'd like her to come over again. I'd be able to do it right this time.

I think I just had to get used to the idea. Everything's so different. And just when "different" was getting to be kind of normal, she came along, and normal became different again. Or different got even more different. Well, something like that. (I'm glad I'm the only one who gets to read this. Nobody else would understand a word of it. I understand it myself though.)

I did tell her, by the way, that I didn't like those nuthouse jokes. She said she'd try not to make jokes like that anymore.

"But why do you do it?" I asked.

"It's just a way of dealing with it."

"But, like about those false teeth, that wasn't funny at all."

"No? Well, I thought it was funny myself. But it's not true, you know. I was exaggerating a lot. They really are all normal, the people there, you know, just like me. People with a few problems they can't manage on their own."

"But you were never on your own, were you? Wasn't I there?"

"Yes, of course you were. But you can't solve my problems for me."

"Why not?"

"Nobody can. I have to do that myself."

"Then why are you over there? If you have to do it by yourself anyway, you might as well be living at home."

"I need a little help."

I decided not to talk about it anymore, even though she kept contradicting herself all the time.

later:

My hair looks good! Johan (the barber) couldn't remember who I was. When I described Uncle Corry, though, he *was* able to remember Uncle Corry. "He's still giving me nightmares," he said (but he smiled when he said that, so it was probably a joke).

"His blind date didn't really turn out," I said.

"Blind date?"

"That's why he was here. He was going on a blind date." I suddenly realized that I hadn't told the barber anything at all about a blind date. I had told the men's clothing man, but not the barber. "A blind date is when you haven't met somebody yet before you have a date with them."

"I know what a blind date is," said Johan.

We got into a conversation about the pros and cons of blind dates. I talked as if I'd had a lot already. We had a real man-to-man discussion. (Rita was sitting off a ways by the waiting-room table, reading magazines, and couldn't hear what we were saying.) Johan really couldn't come up with any advantages. He said they were always a disappointment because you had expectations, but then the reality was different. I said that I liked them because they're exciting. And a blind date can be a lot better in the end, too, like when you imagine she's going to be really ugly and stupid but in reality she's not ugly and stupid.

"So far I've never experienced that," said Johan.

"Me neither," I said. "But it's possible."

"Everything's possible."

Rita thought my hair was awesome too. She said it was a little less dorky. I said, "What do you mean, less dorky? Was it dorky?"

"Kind of," she said. "You know, not very cool."

"So it's cool now?"

"Yeah, I think so, a lot cooler."

Weird word, *cool*. I said it ten times in a row and it kept getting weirder. Rita started saying it, too, and we both thought it was a super-weird word. Cool, cool, cool, we walked around town cooling. People looked at us, but we didn't care.

Cool! We're cool! Cool! Cool! I'd never heard such a weird word, even though at the same time I knew it was just a word, like any other word. (Now that I'm writing it down I'm starting to think it's weird again.)

We sat down on a wall to look at the people walking by. We were amazed that the people all looked different even though they had two eyes, a nose, and a mouth.

"There are at least six billion people in the world," said Rita. "They all look different."

"Except for twins," I said. "The monozygotic ones. They look the same. So it's six billion minus the twins. Well, minus half the twins. That's how many people look different." Then I even thought of triplets and quadruplets, but I didn't bother to say anything about them or it was going to get too complicated.

We tried to imagine how much a billion is. A billion is a thousand million. A million is hard to imagine too. So then we made a thousand times a thousand of that. So, a billion is a thousand times a thousand times a thousand, and then times six. It didn't seem like so many that way—too many to really imagine though. We decided not to think about all those other people anymore and just to look at the people we saw right there. That was a whole lot too.

We started counting how many people were good looking, how many were ugly, and how many normal. Most people were normal. Rita counted a lot more ugly people than I did. That's because she was counting the old people.

"They don't count," I said. "They're old. You can't tell anymore if they're good looking or ugly."

Then we got into a whole discussion about what's old and about what's good looking. We didn't get to the bottom of it. So then we started paying attention to clothes. That was more manageable. It was easier to count what was good looking and ugly and normal.

Good looking: 11.

Ugly: 66?

Normal: 100?

At 100 "normal" we stopped. We figured out that most people are "normal," as far as clothing goes.

"One more time," said Rita. She jumped off the wall, ran off a ways, then walked back. After she had walked past me, she came back again. "So?" she asked.

"So, what?"

"Where do I belong?"

What was I supposed to say to that?! "No clue," I said. "I know you too well."

"Coward. So don't say anything." She pulled me off the wall. "Come on, we're going into a few stores to look at clothes."

I'm just going to keep writing until it's full. Can start in my new journal tomorrow.

"Look, this is where Corry bought his new clothes." I looked inside and saw the men's clothing man standing at the cash register. I waved at him.

He must not have seen me.

"Hi!" I shouted really loudly.

He looked at me and the people waiting at the cash register did too. I waved again. The people lined up at the cash register waved back even though I didn't even know them!

"Do you want to go in?" asked Rita. "It's a boring store."

"Just for a second." I said. "Just to say hi."

We walked into the store. "My uncle was happy with the clothes, you know," I said to the man. "He did a lot of whining, but later on he said he was happy with them."

"Well, um … good," said the man. He gave the people at the cash register a bag. "Enjoy." The people left.

"But the blind date didn't work out," I said.

"Oh, you! That's right, now I remember."

That's great! You stand around in a store for two hours talking with somebody who can't even remember you.

"So, it didn't go very well?" he said.

"No. She thought he was fun and really nice too, but she said that they didn't fit with each other."

"Happens a lot."

"I don't think it was the clothes, though. The clothes were good."

"I'm *sure* it wasn't the clothes," said the man. "If there is something I'm sure of, it's that it wasn't the clothes. It could have been everything else, but not the clothes."

(I'm suddenly thinking that maybe he didn't recognize me because my hair is different now.)

"Or the socks," I said. "The socks were good too."

"There he goes with the socks again," said Rita.

"She doesn't want to believe that socks are important," I told the man.

"I've got to get back to work," he said.

"But it's true, isn't it? About the socks?"

"Yes, it's true. Excuse me." And he was gone.

"You see?" I said to Rita.

"That guy can say anything he wants to. He just wants to sell socks. That's why he said that. Come on, we're out of here."

The whole rest of the afternoon we spent looking at clothes. We tried on caps and hats and put on sunglasses. It was a lot of fun.

When we biked back, Rita said, "Normally I do that with girl-friends. Look at clothes downtown, I mean. I've never done that with a boy before."

"Me neither," I said.

"Boys think it's stupid. They only want to play soccer and stuff."

I'm a bit worried. Is it normal that I thought it was fun? Soccer's fun, too, but there's nobody to play with here, so I don't think about it at all.

—

10:05 p.m.:
I made a dinner salad. It's light, tasty, and refreshing when it's hot out. (That's what it says in *Tasty & Healthy*.) Corry said he felt just like a rabbit with all that green stuff.

"It's healthy," I said. "And light and tastes good."

"It's rabbit food. *Crunch-crunch-crunch!*" Corry started chewing loudly on purpose. "I'm Corry the Crazy Rabbit." He made a funny mouth with teeth and opened his eyes wide. He looked really scary. "And if I eat too much green stuff, I'll turn into … Corry, the Killer Rabbit." He clutched the salad bowl, yanked it toward himself, dropped his face into it, and furiously shoveled one bite after another into his mouth. He growled. "Killer Rabbit!" He stared at me over the bowl. It was really scary!

"Cut it out," I said, but I had to laugh really hard. I tossed a piece of bread at him. "Quit it!"

Corry looked at the bread that had landed beside the salad bowl, stopped chewing, looked at me, and slowly started crawling onto the table. "Killer Rabbit grabs cook. Kill, kill, kill!" A lettuce leaf dangled from his mouth. I yelled, jumped up, and ran through the living room. Corry hopped after me.

After a while we flopped on the couch in hysterics.

I got my cooking pay. Usually I get it on Thursday, but this time I got it Wednesday already.

It was a fun day today.

This is the last page, the end of this journal. Bye, journal! Tomorrow I'll start the new one.

Thursday, August 11

I read my old journal today. Holy cow, I wrote a lot. So much happened. Sometimes I didn't even write everything down. That was just about impossible. It was weird reading everything again. I thought it was fun and not fun at the same time. Some parts I kind of skipped. (I knew more or less what was written in them.) I'd hate to think that somebody might read it someday, all of it. I'll have to come up with a good hiding place—when I'm home again, too.

This morning Corry had a talk with somebody about how he could get back to work. It's not so easy, said the lady. They talked about retraining him. That's when you start learning another profession. They're going to do tests with Corry, to see what he'd like and what he'd be good at. He doesn't know that himself. I don't know that either (for him). Weird that adults don't know things like that either. I thought only kids and teenagers didn't know what they wanted to do yet. (Even though I do.)

He had put on his new clothes. He said they made him feel better during the interview. (He didn't have the socks on. They were still in the laundry basket, he said.)

"That means they'll still be useful," I said.

"I'm sick to death of sitting around the house. I want to get back to work, have people around and stuff. I pretty much let it all slide the past couple of years."

"Doesn't your back bother you anymore?"

"It's not bad, *if* I take it easy, but I can't do heavy work anymore."

"Maybe you could ask if you could work for *Angling and*

Anglers. Write articles about angling and anglers. That's not heavy."

"I'd rather work with my hands."

As if writing's not working with your hands! Sometimes it makes me get a cramp in my hand or wrist or arm.

"Maybe I'll do some volunteer work for a while first. They said that's a good way to get back into the swing of things."

"Doing what?"

"Don't know. Something. I'll see."

"You can look in the paper," I said.

"I don't have a paper."

"Yes you do. You've got that door-to-door advertiser thing. Maybe there's something in there."

"Oh yeah. Good plan."

So he went to check out the ads in the papers that were already in and around the paper-recycling box.

This journal is definitely a lot thinner than my old one. I wanted the fat one, really. It was nicer looking, too, but cost an awful lot. When it's my birthday, I'll ask for a new fat one. That's still a long way off, though, so until that time I'll just have to write a little smaller. And just try again to write everything a little shorter. Maybe from now on nothing much will happen.

I also debated getting one of those journals with a lock, but anyhow they're too small and too girlish and then it just seems so … well, like I've got a diary. Too bad, though, because having a lock is handy.

I'm going to the park. Luckily Corry has a soccer ball in one of his closets.

evening:

It's not much fun playing soccer by yourself. So I went over to Rita's to see if she wanted to play. She did. I didn't think it was all that much fun, though, because she's better at it than I am. I was scared the whole time that somebody would see. (A lot of people walked by, with dogs and stuff.) Why is Rita always better at sports than I am? I want to be better at something too. I wish I could play chess. If I could play chess well, I'm sure I'd be better at it than she would be. I remembered that I was going to ask Jaap if he wanted to teach me. (I know he can play because he told me that once.)

After playing soccer, she asked if I'd go with her to Pete's tomorrow night.

"What for?" I asked.

"We're going to look at the takes of my interview with Aunt Gea," she said.

"Oh." That's great! She just went ahead and filmed without me.

"You didn't show up and Gea was going to be on vacation this week, so then I called Pete to see if I could borrow his camera. He said okay, except he wanted to be the one to use it."

"Oh."

"You want to come?"

"I don't know. I wanted to ask your dad if he'd teach me how to play chess. I want to learn how to play."

"I could do that. I play chess a lot with my dad. Why don't you go with me. I can teach you how to play chess later."

"Well, okay."

Crap.

Friday, August 12

My mom called this afternoon. She asked if I thought it was fun having her there.

"Yes," I said, "a lot of fun."

"I'm not coming this weekend, though. Suddenly I thought maybe now Maurits is hoping I'll come again this weekend. But I'm not coming."

"That's all right."

"Maybe another time, but not now. I don't know how things are."

"It's up to you."

"I was really glad to see you. Things are okay over there? With Uncle Corry?"

"Yes, he's fine. He's going back to work. He's been meeting with somebody. They're going to do tests."

"I meant with *you* and Corry. But I don't understand, isn't he working?"

"No, he has back trouble."

"Oh, I thought he was over that a long time ago."

"No. Maybe he'll be working at the fix-it library. He's got a meeting this afternoon."

"Fix-it library?"

"Yeah, it's just like a library, but with tools instead of books. You can become a member and then borrow all kinds of tools—ladders and drills and pliers and lots more stuff. It's a volunteer job."

Corry ran across an ad yesterday in the advertiser paper from six months back. He called and they said that at that moment they didn't especially need anybody, but he was always welcome to stop in for a chat. They needed new people regularly, so who knows, maybe he could get on file.

"A volunteer job? Doesn't sound like something for Corry. And how are things with you?"

"Fine." And suddenly I blurted it out. "Mom, what's the situation with Dad? What if he comes back before you're back? Am I supposed to live with him?" (I didn't bring up Florrie's name.)

It was quiet on the other end of the line.

"Mom, I want to know. Am I supposed to stay here? I'd prefer to go to my own school."

It stayed quiet. "So, do you want to live with him?" she asked after a while.

"Well, *want* to … I don't know what I want. I just want to go to my own school when it's time."

"Can't you stay at Steven's?"

"No. No way. I don't want to stay at Steven's."

"Oh, well, but maybe I'll be back already by then."

"But maybe not!" I shouted into the receiver. "It's not a long way off!" I was suddenly so fed up. Why didn't she just say something? Why do I have to come up with everything myself?

I heard her nose-snuffling.

"Forget it," I said. "Just forget it. We'll see."

"Yes," she said in a high little voice. "We'll see. It'll be all right, honest. Don't worry. I don't want you to worry."

"But I *do* worry," I said. "Sorry, but I can't help it. I just happen to think about that sometimes."

"You're such a sweetie," she said. "And you can't do a thing about any of this either."

"No."

"But that would be a real surprise."

"What?"

"Well, that he'd suddenly come back right now."

"Who?"

"Him. Why would he suddenly come back right now?"

"Why not?" I said. "It would be surprising if he *didn't* suddenly come back right now. Why wouldn't he come back? It's only a couple of hours by plane."

"Oh. Well."

"It's possible, isn't it?"

"I'll call you again, really soon. We'll talk more. I have to go eat in a minute."

We hung up. I do feel kind of rotten that I brought up my dad. But I felt rotten when I *didn't* bring him up. Except that was a different kind of rotten, not less or worse, just different. I simply wanted to know, so I asked—except I still don't know anything.

Well, maybe he'll be gone for months even—or a year. It's possible.

I'm going to figure out how long he's been gone already. In January he went to Florrie's. In March they left on their trip—no, in April. It was April 5. I remember because Steven's birthday was two days before. So, he's been traveling for over four months now.

later:

I'm glad I brought it up.

Made navy beans with all kinds of stuff mixed in.

The talk Corry had with the fix-it library went really well. He had his new clothes on again. They'd love to have him because he's handy and knows a lot about tools. He can give people advice too. He said he'd worked construction and they thought that was a big plus. He didn't say he really only did bricklaying and so doesn't know a lot about other things. He knows next to nothing about, like, plumbing, but he said that didn't matter. He's handy and he learns quickly. Next week he's going to do a shift as a trial run. I'm happy for him.

evening:
Corry wasn't there when I got home. After half an hour he showed up. He'd been to the café. He cursed at all the people over there again. They had laughed at him because he was going to do volunteer work. They thought that was something for bored housewives.

I asked, "Why do you still go there? I thought you didn't want to go there anymore."

He said he didn't want to sit at home all the time. He wanted to get out once in a while.

Me: "So, you go somewhere else."

Him: "I won't know anybody if I go somewhere else."

Me: "So, you can get to know them, can't you? Maybe people somewhere else are more fun."

Him: "Maybe. Well, I'll see. Jesus, I'm sick of that crowd."

Then he tottered off to bed. He'd had a lot to drink again. I don't get why some people drink alcohol. It doesn't make them any more fun to be around.

It was really nice at Pete and Alied and Eva's. Eva's brother Harold was there too. He'd been on vacation out on Terschelling, camping on the island with friends. He told lots of stories. I'd like to go to Terschelling too, sometime. It sounds like fun.

The interview with Gea was pretty good. Actually I was secretly hoping that it wouldn't be good and that they'd say, "We need you, Rits. We can't do it without you."

By the way, it turns out that Pete and Alied already donated twenty euros toward the movie. I didn't know about that! Rita already bought some videotapes herself.

In the video, Gea said a lot about Rita's mom, about when she was a girl. I'm not going to write all that down because it's on the tape.

I feel like I want to keep going with that movie again, even though at first I didn't really feel like it at all.

Tomorrow we're going swimming. It's supposed to be a beautiful day, they say.

Saturday, August 13

Danny was there, too, at the pond. I saw him walking up. I scooched over a little behind Rita and tried to make myself small, but it was too late. He'd seen me. "So, here's the great Mr. Filmmaker who has to be paid a bundle for his brilliant video work. Except it's too bad that our great Mr. Filmmaker here doesn't show up to do any filming."

"I couldn't make it," I said.

"No, your mommy showed up. You can't go anywhere, huh, if your mommy's around."

"Cut it out," I said. "You don't know what's going on. It was important. I really couldn't make it."

"What?" said Rita. "I don't get it. That was Saturday, wasn't it, when your mother came? Were you going to film The Geeks too? You were supposed to go with *me* to film."

To make a long story short, Rita and Danny were both mad at me again. I had accidentally made double arrangements. I'd forgotten all about that.

Luckily Eva jumped in, saying to Danny, "What difference does it make? He'll just film you guys some other time." ("Well, we don't have gigs that often," said Danny. "Not in the middle of the summer anyway. The next one won't be for a month.") And to Rita, she said, "You got to film with Dad, didn't you? Everything went fine, didn't it?"

"That's not the point," said Rita.

"What is the point?" asked Eva.

"Well, you know … oh, forget it."

"Who's going in?" asked Eva.

"I am," I said.

"Me too," said Rita.

Dachsy joined us. Danny didn't. He kept on walking.

I don't think he would want to give me his old drum set now or sell it to me cheap.

"I'd rather learn from Jaap," I said to Rita. We were drying out in the sun. (I'm pretty brown already!)

"What?" she asked.

"Chess. It's more for men."

Rita and Eva burst out giggling (a typical girl's sputter).

"Listen to *him*," said Rita.

And Eva said, "If it's for *men*, then why do *you* want to do it?" They sputtered even harder.

"Well, you know what I mean," I said. "For guys."

"What makes you think that?" asked Rita.

"Like, you know, because." Why can't something just be the way it is? Why does there always have to be a reason for something? "Some things just are the way they are," I concluded. "No reason."

"If you fall down the stairs, you're downstairs in a hurry," said Eva.

"Exactly," I said. "If you fall down the stairs, you're downstairs in a hurry. There's no reason for it. It's just the way it is."

"There is a reason for it though," said Rita. "It's because of gravity. If there were no gravity, you wouldn't fall."

"But even so, you can fall without a reason," I said. "Somebody might push you, but you can also fall just like that."

"Not," said Rita. "There's always a reason. You don't just fall. You fall because maybe you lose your balance."

"Not necessarily," I said. "You can also just fall because you feel like it or because you don't feel like staying on your feet."

"Then *that's* the reason," said Rita. "If you feel like it, that's a reason too. You see? There's always a reason."

"But you can feel like falling without having a reason for it."

"Not so."

It kept going like that for a long time. I didn't think it was a fun conversation. Rita always wants to be right. And then the worst thing was that at the end she said that *I* always want to be right. "Just admit that you're wrong," she said. "Then you're off the hook. You're not going to win anyway."

"There are two of you," I said. "That's why." And then I walked Dachsy around the pond.

"Did you go away on vacation?" Eva was asking Rita.

"No," said Rita. "I always go in the winter with my dad. We go skiing."

"How about you?" Eva asked me.

"I'm not going this year," I said. "I'm already here on a kind of vacation."

"So when are you going home?" she asked.

"Maybe he'll stay here," said Rita. "Maybe he'll go to my school."

"Well, I don't know," I said. "I'll see how things go."

"So where are your parents?" asked Eva.

"My father's traveling and my mother ..."

A silence fell. Rita and Eva stared at me.

"She's, um ..."

Suddenly I'd had enough. Why shouldn't I just say it? What was going to happen if I said it? Was the world going to come crashing down? It really wasn't.

"She's been away for a while," I said. "She was stressed out. Well, a bit worse than that. Not crazy or anything, just, you know ... she had to rest for a while. And now she's in one of those places, an uh ..."

They were still staring at me.

"A kind of ... institution clinic. Not for crazy people, just, you know, one of those buildings where people stay for a while until everything's all right again and they can go home."

"Geez," said Eva.

"Oh," said Rita. "I was thinking it was something like that."

"It's not hereditary, though, or contagious. There's nothing wrong with me."

"Sure, we understand," said Rita.

"I've got an uncle in an institution," said Eva. "He lives there. One of my dad's brothers. He's mentally handicapped."

"My mother's not mentally handicapped," I said. "And she's not living there. She's staying there for a while. She just had a few too many problems, so she had to go there for a while and I went to Uncle Corry's."

Again it was quiet for a time. "Geez," said Eva.

Eva and Rita were very nice to me the rest of the afternoon— almost *too* nice, as if there were something so terrible going on with me that they couldn't be jerks anymore, like before, with that talk about chess and falling down the stairs.

I'd rather have that conversation, if I could choose. I almost felt sorry I'd said anything.

The good thing, though, is that Rita called an hour ago to see if I could come by tonight. Jaap was home too. He wouldn't mind teaching me chess, she said.

She didn't bring up again that she'd do it. I'm going over to see them in a minute.

Sunday, August 14

I can play chess! Not very well yet, but after a couple of hours it was already getting better. Now I know all the rules at least.

Today Rita is going over to see her girlfriend who just got back from vacation. The girlfriend called last night while I was playing chess with Jaap. I'm curious whether Rita still wants to do much with me now that her friend is back. She had asked me to come along that first time only because she was bored.

I don't have anything to do all day today, no plans, I mean. Corry's gone too. He went fishing. He asked me if I wanted to go, but I didn't. Fishing's not fun at all, certainly not for the fish. Corry says it doesn't make any difference to the fish because they can't feel and, on top of that, he throws them back again after he's caught them. He can't eat them. The canal's much too dirty.

"How do you know they can't feel?" I asked.

"You can just tell," he said. "They're dumb animals."

"Just because they're dumb doesn't mean they can't feel," I said. "You ..." I swallowed a nasty (but good!) comment at the last moment. "It doesn't seem like much fun to me being on a hook."

"Then they shouldn't go and hang themselves on one. They do it themselves."

That suddenly reminds me of what Eva said. She overheard a conversation between her mom and Petra. Petra had said she thought Corry was nice enough, but pretty boorish. She was looking more for a man who liked theater and good music and that kind of thing—the type you can go see a museum with (from the inside, too, she meant) when you're on vacation, instead of only drinking beer on a café terrace.

The word *boorish* does fit Corry, although I think he's changed (maybe not enough yet for Petra though). Or maybe he's somebody you just have to get to know a little better before you think he's nice. I think he's nice (in spite of the fact that he's boorish sometimes).

I feel like doing something fun.

later:
Booooooooooooooooooooooooooooooooooooooooooooooooooo oooooooooooooooooooooooooooored.

later:
Booooₒₒ°ooooooooRED

later:
I'm bored. I keep wanting to write because it's the only thing I can think of doing, but then when I sit here, I don't feel like it and I can't think of anything to write.

later:
I biked downtown, but it was boring there too. All the stores were closed. There were a lot of people sitting on café terraces. Suddenly something weird started to bother me. I didn't dare go by them. I was scared they'd start classifying me into good looking, ugly, or normal. (They wouldn't classify me as "good looking," I'm sure, not even as "normal," I thought.) So then I just went home again.

I looked in the bathroom mirror for a while and at first couldn't really discover much that was weird. The longer I looked, though, the weirder I seemed. Do I look like my father or like my mother? (Like neither one as far as I can tell.) How long will it take before I start growing a beard? How tall will I get? Am I going to grow more? What if I always stay the way I am now? (Rita's already taller than I am, even though she's almost five months younger!) What will I look like if I have to wear glasses? (My dad has glasses.) What if I never meet a girl who thinks I'm cool?

Well, that last thing might not be so bad. Maybe it is, I don't know. I don't need to get involved with girls, but maybe it would be cool if they thought I was cool. For a while I thought I liked Eva. I wasn't in love, like Rita kept saying, but I did want her to think *I* was cool. Later that feeling went away though. A lot of the time she acts so busy and theatrical. But then, she's eight months younger than I am. I think it's best after all to like somebody your own age.

My mom didn't do that—like somebody her own age, I mean. My dad is three years younger than she is, even though when you're that old maybe it doesn't make much of a difference anymore. It's still a weird idea. When my dad was as old as I am, my mom was sixteen already! They didn't know each other then, though. It wasn't until a lot later, when they were in their twenties or something, that they got to know each other.

I wish I knew where they met. It was somewhere here in the city because they both lived here. Maybe they even walked down this street and saw the window of the room I'm in right now without knowing I would ever be sitting here because they didn't even know I was going to exist. It's a weird idea to think they *already* existed and were doing all kinds of things before I was around—before they knew that I would ever come.

What if that little sister hadn't died? I would have had a sister named Emma now. Maybe I would have sat here with her. She would have been eight or something.

But that's not how it is.

There's no little sister, my dad's with Florrie on a trip around the world, my mom's in that institution thing, and Corry's fishing. That's how it is, period. I could sit around all the time wishing it wasn't like this, but that doesn't help. It doesn't make things any different. (That Corry's fishing isn't a bad thing in itself obviously.) (Well, except for the fish.)

Funny, I feel a little better all of a sudden. That horrible feeling of boredom is gone, I think. I'm really going to do something now. (I still don't know what.)

evening:

I went for a bike ride. I came to an industrial park and there were lots of businesses there where they sell cars. I looked at the cars and picked one I'd buy if I had money (and a driver's license). It was a big red one. There were other nice-looking cars, but the red one was the shiniest, although I couldn't even really see all the cars. I had to look inside through the plate-glass windows because the businesses were closed.

When I got home, Corry had already gotten back. He hadn't caught much but had talked a long time with another fisherman. He said that was different because anglers usually don't talk a lot with each other. I said then maybe it was time for him to take up another sport.

"How come?" he asked.

"Then you can talk more," I said.

"About what?"

"About all kinds of stuff. Then you'll get to know new people."

He didn't think it was a very good idea. He didn't really like sports (except watching soccer on TV).

It's already mid-August. I have to come up with what I'm supposed to do. School's going to start again. I don't feel like it at all—like school or like coming up with stuff. I think it's stupid that you absolutely have to go to school until you're sixteen. Why do you have to if you already know what you want to be anyway? I not only *know* what I want to be, I already *am* what I want to be. So why do I have to learn all kinds of things I don't need?

What is cool, though, is that when school starts, I won't be the youngest and the shortest one there anymore. Other kids are going to be the youngest and the shortest. If I go to school here, though, I'll have to start all over again anyhow. Well, not all over, because I'll already know Rita (Eva's at another school). Rita's a girl, though, and that doesn't do me much good. I'm sure she's going to do things with her girlfriends all the time and then I'll be alone. So I do want to go to my own school. Steven and all the other kids will be there.

I'm going to ask Uncle Corry how we're going to go about the school thing. Why should I come up with everything myself? Let him come up with something for a change.

Monday, August 15

Uncle Corry said he wouldn't mind calling my old school and my (maybe) new school. He had no clue either about how those kinds of things are supposed to be arranged, although he did think I'd have to go to school here. I could hardly live at home on my own.

"Why not?" I asked.

He didn't have a good answer to that. "Because. Kids of thirteen don't live on their own. That's the way it is."

"*Because* isn't a reason."

"Well, uh … what happens if you get sick?"

"What happens if *you* get sick? You live on your own too."

"You don't have any money."

"I'll go work," I said. "Or I'll ask my mom for money."

"She won't allow you to live on your own."

"Why not?"

"Because. Kids of thirteen don't live on their own."

Actually I don't want to go live on my own at all. I still don't get why it wouldn't be allowed, though, if I wanted to. What is it, then, exactly that adults *can* do that somebody who's thirteen can't? I can do everything adults can as far as I know—like cooking. If you couldn't do that, I can imagine you wouldn't be allowed to live by yourself. I can cook though. Who came up with the idea that you have to be eighteen or something before you can live on your own? Do you suddenly know everything that you're supposed to know then? As far as I can tell, I already know everything you're supposed to know. On top of that, it would be for just a short time because my mom's coming home again soon anyway. Until then, I can ask Mrs. B if I don't know something. She's sixty already or seventy, so I'm sure she'll know everything.

Oh, well, it doesn't matter. I'd rather stay here, I think, than go live on my own, even though I'll have to go to another school.

I was just thinking. I don't know how the washing machine works, although I'm sure it's not really that hard to learn.

I called Tineke, but she wasn't there. They said she was going to be out all week. That really sucks! She just takes off without saying anything. I don't know what I'm supposed to do now. I'm not going to do anything for a while. I'll figure something out.

You know what I think is so weird? There must have been all kinds of things wrong between my parents, but they never got into any arguments. I never noticed anything anyway. They usually acted really normal. I think. My mom did get mad a lot if my dad or I made a mess, but other than that she usually didn't. My dad never got mad. He usually didn't say very much. I tend to talk a lot and my mom, too, but my dad doesn't. Actually we never did much together, not like Rita, for example. She does all kinds of things with her dad, plays chess or other games. Or Eva, she also does stuff with her dad. (As far as I can tell, though, Steven doesn't do much with his dad either—maybe it's more a girl thing, that a girl tends to do lots of things with her dad.)

My dad let me see old pictures once. That was at the beginning of January, a couple of weeks before he left (to go to Florrie's). I didn't even know those pictures existed! They were pictures of him as a teenager and of later on when he was in his twenties. They were all in a shoebox. They weren't glued into albums like the other pictures, the ones with my mom and me in them. I thought it was cool to see those old pictures.

"That was me, back when," he said. "Different, huh?"

Very different—in some of them he had a little beard! And really weird hair. He looked awful. I think my mom would have run away screaming if she had seen him then.

He told me who the other people in the pictures were. He had a lot of friends back in those days. I can remember that I thought it was weird that he suddenly told me so much. He even told me about girlfriends he had had, although he also told me that he *really* fell in love only when he got to know my mom (with her, that is). He thought my mom was tremendous and very beautiful and special. I didn't really want to hear it. It gave me an uncomfortable ashamed feeling, but on the other hand it *was* cool to hear. When I heard him talking like that, I thought: I know for sure that they're never going to get divorced the way some other parents I know have.

Chess with Rita this afternoon.

evening:

Crap. She really can play better than I can, although that's because she's been doing it for years already and I just started. After three games she didn't want to play anymore. She thought it was boring because she was able to win so easily. So then we played Monopoly. She won that too (but not as easily).

She asked if I knew yet if I was going to her school. I said I didn't.

"So, when will you know?" she asked.

I didn't know that either.

"You don't know very much," she said.

At that point I got fed up. People who always win at games and then, on top of that, act like you're dumb are not fun to be around.

11:23 p.m.:

I was just lying down thinking of all kinds of things—like my dad rescuing that pigeon from the water last summer. Back then I thought that was really fantastic, but now I'm suddenly thinking why rescue a pigeon and then go and leave your kid to rot?

11:46 p.m.:

I was just lying down thinking: they have nothing to do with each other, that he rescued the pigeon and that he left. It *was* great that he did that (rescue the pigeon, I mean). I didn't dare, myself. I was scared. The pigeon was struggling so hard. My dad stepped into the (dirty) water just like that!

Tuesday, August 16

I'm going to school here.

Last night in bed I thought about it. My dad really isn't going to happen to come back just in time, and if he does come back I won't know what's going to happen anyway. In any event, I don't feel like living with that Florrie woman (*if* she even allowed me to).

When I woke up this morning, I called my mom. Of course I didn't get her on the phone this time either. They said she was busy. I told them she had to call back as soon as possible. After a couple of hours she did. I said, "School's starting again on Monday."

"Oh," she said. "School. Oh, right."

As if she still hadn't thought about it at all!—even though I'd told her before.

"What am I supposed to do?" I asked. "I wouldn't mind going home, but then I'd have to have money to buy food and stuff and school things."

"Are you nuts? You're not going to live at home all by yourself!"

"Why not?"

"That's just not possible."

"Why not?"

"Kids don't live on their own. It's just not possible."

"What am I supposed to do, then? School's going to start."

It was quiet for a while. I listened to the sound of the phone line and thought it's never *really* quiet on the phone. You always hear something. Is it ever really quiet anywhere? You'll always hear something, a breath, a little sigh, a creak, a footstep. (I heard all those things during the "silence.")

"Maybe you should go to school *there* for a while," she said. "For a little while, not very long."

"But how does that get arranged? Aren't you supposed to call or something? Am I the one who's supposed to report in?"

"Is Corry there? Could I talk with him for a minute?"

To make a long story short: my mom and Corry are now going to arrange it. I don't know exactly what they're going to do and how. I don't understand it all exactly, but then I also don't feel like understanding it.

I don't think it's much fun that, on the one hand, I *do* have to come up with everything and say it myself and, on the other, I'm not allowed to live on my own. She never brings up those kinds of things, problems and sticky situations. I'm always the one who has to bring them up, but then everything I say and come up with isn't any good.

Now Rita wants to do everything with Pete's camera! Tonight we're going to film her uncle Dirk. Pete's going too. I was allowed to come along but only as an assistant. Huh? Assistant? So I said that. I said, "Huh? Assistant?"

Her: "Pete knows how to do it better than you do. It has to be a good movie."

Me: "Well, that's great. It was my idea, and now suddenly I can only be the assistant."

Her: "What do you mean, your idea? It was my idea."

Me: "It was my idea to make a movie about your mother."

Her: "How on earth did you come up with that? It was my own idea."

Me: "No it wasn't. I remember exactly. You were staying over at

Gea and Arend's and I stopped by and that's when I said that the whole story about your mother was good material for a movie." I remembered it very well because I had read through that part only a few days ago.

Her: "I can't remember any of that."

Me (and my stupid mouth): "I can, and I've got proof. I wrote it down!" I wanted to snatch the words back and swallow them, but that was impossible. Crap. Nobody's supposed to know I have a journal. And *if* they do happen to know (like Rita), I want them to forget. On top of that, now that whole issue about her reading it got stirred up again too!! Sure enough:

Her: "In that diary of yours, I'll bet."

Me: "Well, it's not really a—"

Her: "That's no proof. I can write down all kinds of stuff, too, but that doesn't prove that it's true. I could write down that I flew to the moon, but that doesn't make it so."

Me: "It's not a diary. It's just a journal. I write things down, exactly the way they happened."

Her: "A diary. I have a diary, too, and it says something totally different."

Rita, a diary? She doesn't seem at all like the diary type to me.

"Okay, let me read it," I said.

"No frigging way!"

We kept on quarreling about it for a while longer and in the end she was willing to admit that she had hit on the idea because of me, because I was working on the video and making movies, not because I had said anything. And: victory! I *can* be the cameraman. Pete's coming to keep an eye on his things, to focus the camera and turn it on and off and stuff. He can make sure that everything gets on film right and he can think along about what kind of shots we're going to shoot. But for the rest, I'm doing it. So, actually that makes him the assistant.

I told Rita about the school decision.
    I said, "I know now."
    "What do you know?"
    "If I'm going to your school or not."
    "Oh. And?"
    I let a silence fall to stretch the suspense.
    "So, tell me."
    "Would you like it if I went?"
    "Not if you're going to be stupid like you are now."
    "I'm going to go to your school."
    "Oh." She didn't cheer or jump up and down or anything, but I believe she thought it was cool anyway. She started telling me about everybody in her class, who's stupid and who's good at sports and who's not. There were so many names that I didn't remember a single one.

I'm glad I know now, but just the same I TOTALLY don't feel like going. I thought it was bad enough last year—a new school and (almost) all new kids. Steven was the only one I actually knew in my class, but we weren't really friends yet then. It took a long time before I felt even a little comfortable. Things kept getting better, though, and at the end of the year I had quite a lot of friends (Steven being the best one) and guys I could hang around with. Now I have to start all over again. Crap. I don't even know if it's a nice school or not, Rita's school. I'm going only because I know *one* person there at least. Of course, I could go to Eva's school, too, if it's better, because I know one person there too (Eva). Well, it doesn't matter. It's probably just for a little while anyway. For a little while I can keep it up, even if it's not a nice school. I'll just have to.

Wednesday, August 17

I had an awesome idea yesterday. Right before I went over to Rita's to go to Pete's to go to Dirk's, I thought: I'm going to take my camera, too, just in case. You never know. Maybe Pete's will break and I can save the day by having a camera with me. On top of that, of course, a real cameraman never leaves home without his camera (except if he's going to do something totally different from filming, like swimming or going to the library). Then as I was riding my bike on the sidewalk to Rita's house, I got an even more awesome idea.

I'm going to make "The making of"!

They do that a lot. I've seen all kinds of "making ofs" on TV. That's when you see how they made the movie. Like you see the director and the cameraman at work and the actors when they're not. Really cool.

I'm going to call my movie *The Making of Anneke*, because Rita's mom was called Anneke and so is the movie that Rita's making. Now it doesn't feel so bad that she wanted to have all the ideas and asked Pete to join in. I'll just make my own movie! I realized that I would also have to be in it and that I'd be interviewed about my movie and how I came up with the idea and stuff—at which point I can say that the movie *Anneke* was really my idea. (I'll have to make sure Rita's not the interviewer, or we'll start another argument.) (Ha, ha, I'll just do it in the mirror again!)

I turned the camera on and rang Rita's doorbell. She opened the door and asked what I was doing for crying out loud. I told her.

She said it was all very nice and so on, but she didn't want to be in the movie. I said, "You'll have to be because that's exactly what it's about. This is *The Making of.*"

We biked over to Pete's. Pete thought it was a cool plan. That way I'd have a good opportunity to practice filming. "But it *will* be more work this way," he said, "because it'll all still have to be edited." I said that didn't matter. (This conversation is on the tape too.)

I've got a lot of takes already:

— Rita who opens the door and doesn't want to be in the movie
— Eva who opens the door and does want to be in the movie
— Pete who says it's a cool idea
— On our way in the car to Dirk's
— Dirk who opens the door and walks ahead of us down the hall
— The whole interview with Dirk, plus Rita who asks questions and Pete who's filming
— Rita who says that I have to quit filming her
— Lots of other shots, including bottles of beer, Dirk's ears, Rita's hands, her notepad with questions, Pete's back, Dirk's girlfriend with the shrill voice who comes and goes a lot.

The interview with Dirk I didn't follow much. I had to pay attention to my own movie. On the way back, I asked if we couldn't do the interview with Gea again. That has to be in *The Making of Anneke* too, I think, and I missed it because my mom was here.

Rita said that I shouldn't be so ridiculous. It was okay for me to make my movie (Aha! She thinks it *is* a good idea), but then I shouldn't mess around in *her* movie.

Actually I think this movie is going to be better than Rita's. As far as I can tell, hers is going to be pretty boring.

Everything's going along fine again. I'm glad I finally know what's what about school. I'm still not looking forward to it, but it's better than not knowing and having to be unsure about what's what. I'm also glad that I'm filming again. That way I've got something really cool to do and maybe I'll finally start writing less too. I don't know anymore why I ever thought I might want to be a writer. Making movies is much more fun! Writing's fun, too, but there's always so much to write that you get tired and your hand cramps up. Filming makes you less tired because you only have to look through the lens. (If you do it for a really long time, though, you *will* get a cramped shoulder and a cramped eye.) Well, what's important is that, as far as I can tell, I'm really good at filming. Everybody can write things down, but not everybody can make movies! You have to have talent for that.

later:
Postcard from Steven. It came in the mail this afternoon. Mrs. B sent it on to me in an envelope. When I saw the envelope, my heart kind of lurched. For a second, I thought there might be a card from my dad in it, but obviously it turned out there wasn't.

He wrote: "Hi. Are you already home again? Don't eat too much ice cream. Steven." On the front, there's a picture of a really fat man with an ice-cream cone who has fallen through a beach chair.

evening:
Uncle Corry worked at the fix-it library. It went well, he said, and

it was also pretty fun. A woman came in, for example, and she knew nothing about doing repairs. Her husband had always done that, but he was dead, so now she wanted to learn to do it herself because she had a house that needed a lot of little repairs (she didn't want to learn the big jobs herself). Corry was able to tell her all kinds of things about drills and stuff. (She had come to borrow one.) I asked if he had gotten a date with the lady at the same time. She doesn't have a husband now, so maybe she'd want to go with Corry.

"She was much too old," he said.

"How old?"

"A hundred and twenty or something."

"Wow, and she still wants to repair things?"

"Well, sixty maybe. Too old, at any rate."

"By the way, how old are you?"

"Forty-two."

"That's old too," I said. "So what difference does it make?"

Corry thought it did make a difference. He wanted a woman of about his own age, not a lot younger because that made for problems, and not a lot older either.

Is three years a lot? I don't think so if you're already that old, but maybe it is. My parents are three years apart (almost three and a half) and they had problems too.

Thursday, August 18

Why why why why why why why why why why why why why
why does everything go the way it does???

Why why why why why why why why doesn't anything ever
go the way I want it to for a little while??? Don't feel like writing.

Why why why and that times a thousand times a thousand
times a thousand.

Friday, August 19

So, my dad's been back almost two weeks already. I'm really glad he's back.

evening:
No. Don't feel like it.

Saturday, August 20

8:00 in the morning

I'll just have to for a little while. I'll try to write everything as short as possible.

They had just gotten to Mexico. Florrie called her mother. The call was forwarded to her sister. It turned out that Florrie's mother was in the hospital for an operation. Florrie wanted to go home right away. My dad went with her.

Why did Florrie call her mother and my dad not call me? Obviously he didn't know I was here, but when I was still at home he didn't call either.

He's coming over this afternoon.

It's so stupid. The whole time I've been here, I've been hoping he'd come back, and now that he's here, I wish he had stayed away a little longer.

Corry asked, "What are you going to do now? Are you going to live with him?"

"I don't know."

He was quiet for a long time. Corry looked out the window. He scratched at a spot on the glass, but it was on the outside. "It's okay with me if you stay here, you know," he said.

"Oh."

"Up to you. I'm just saying it."

"Okay."

Does it all have to be up to me *again*? I don't want it to be up to me. As far as I can see, it doesn't make sense that all those things have to be up to you when you're thirteen.

On the phone, my dad said he had kept trying to call to say that he was back but nobody answered the phone at home. He had called every day, he said. He thought Mom and I were probably on vacation. It was only after a week that he started getting (a little) worried, because my mom doesn't like vacations and never wants to go away for longer than a week (preferably not at all). Then he thought that maybe I had gone with Steven and his family.

"And Mom, what about her?" I asked. "Where did you think she was?"

He didn't know. (He didn't know what he thought.)

After a while he finally decided to call a few people (friends and acquaintances of *his*). Nobody knew anything about it. He hadn't thought of Mrs. B. Then he ran into her by accident downtown. She told him that my mom had been "gone a time" and that I was staying with my uncle. That was Wednesday. (He called Thursday morning.)

"And now?" I asked.

"*What* now?"

"That's what I'm asking you. What now?"

He didn't know what now. He said he'd really prefer to get back to his trip, but it depended on Florrie's mother. He saw this as a kind of stopover because the trip wasn't done yet.

I wonder why it depends on Florrie's mother and not on me.

Obviously I told him about Mom. He was taken aback. He asked how long she'd been there already.

"Starting June 16," I said.

"Really! That's long. So there's really something wrong, then."

"What to do you mean 'really something wrong'?"

"Well, you know. It'll be bad, I mean."

"Could be worse. It's already a lot better."

"And all this time you've been at Corry's?"

"Yes. Well, almost. At first I stayed at Steven's for a while, until vacation started. They were going to France."

"Couldn't you go with them?"

"No."

"And when's your mother coming back, then?"

"I don't know."

Then he told me the whole story about trying to call and all.

I wonder what would have happened if he hadn't accidentally run into Mrs. B downtown. Would he never have found out that I'm here? Or would he just have left again whenever Florrie's mother was all better? At the end of our talk, he said he had to let everything settle and had to talk with Florrie. He would call me back tomorrow (Friday, so yesterday).

He didn't call until that night, even though I stayed home the whole day. He said he would come by tomorrow (so today) to talk. He couldn't tell me an exact time. It depended on a number of things, he said.

That sucks. So, I can sit here again and do nothing but wait.

11:15 a.m.:

Rita just called to ask if I wanted to go swimming with her and Eva and Lisa (that girlfriend of Rita's who was on vacation at first). "I can't," I said. (Cool that she asked me, in spite of Lisa's being back again.)

Then she asked if I was going to go tonight. She was going to interview her aunt Alied for the movie.

I said I didn't know yet. I told her that my dad was coming.

"Oh, so he's back?"

"Looks like."

"You don't sound very enthusiastic."

"I am."

"So you're not going to go to school here anymore."

"I don't know."

"Why not?"

"I don't know what's going to happen. My dad wants to go away again."

"How weird."

"What do you mean 'weird'?"

"He's your father, isn't he? My father stayed here to take care of me when my mother was dying. He didn't go sailing anymore."

"My father will stay too, if he has to, you know! We just don't know! And *my* mother isn't dead!"

"Hey, calm down."

"I'll call you." I quickly hung up.

Crap.

I don't feel at all like sitting around here and waiting. I feel like going swimming. I wish everything were normal.

12:40 p.m.:

I almost cried just now. I didn't feel like it so I didn't, but I felt like shit just the same.

It's not fun at all. I haven't seen him in four and a half months already and I really feel like seeing him. He's been gone for four and a half months! I'm incredibly glad he's back. Why does it all feel so weird and so not fun?

I wonder what Florrie's mother has. Who knows, maybe she'll die. Seems it's bad enough to come home all the way from Mexico for. You don't do that for something that's not bad. Why does everybody keep dying? Dying doesn't seem fun at all to me. I don't want to think about it. They say that everybody dies sometime, but until a little while ago I always knew for sure it would never happen to me. I don't get why it has to either.

And why do people want to have kids if you already know that they're going to die someday? That's not fun at all, is it? You've just had a baby but you already know that it's going to die. Usually not right away, of course, like my little sister, maybe only after eighty years, but it'll happen someday. I'll never want to have kids.

Sunday, August 21

Going to do just a little writing because this thinking's driving me crazy. Thinking gives me headaches.

I've been lying in bed all morning already and for a little while I was scared I wouldn't be able to walk anymore. I wasn't really paralyzed or anything, but it seemed kind of like it was the beginning. It wasn't *really* bad, but it felt like it might get bad really quick. Everything weighed a ton—my arms, my legs, my whole body. I imagined I had to have a wheelchair.

Now that I'm sitting up to write, it's already a little less bad. Corry came in an hour ago to see what had happened to me. I told him I couldn't get out of bed and that everything felt so weird. He said I just had to get my butt out next to the bed and it would turn out nothing was wrong.

I said I'd do that.

SCHOOL BEGINS TOMORROW, BUT WHERE AM I SUPPOSED TO GO???!!!

Couldn't he have come before? Or later? Why right now? Why why why?

I'd much rather go to my own school. When that was impossible, it wasn't such a problem. It just wasn't possible. Now it is possible, except I'll have to live with my dad and that Florrie woman for a while in that little house. I don't feel like it.

My dad said yesterday that at first it hadn't seemed like such a good idea to him for me to come live with them. Her little house was really too cramped for two people as it was, but Florrie had told him she thought it would be okay. We would all just have to take up less room and then it would be fine. It would only be for a little while, until my mother was back. My dad wants to go away again as soon as possible. As it turned out, though, when he talked with Florrie about it she actually thought it was nice to be back home. She doesn't want to leave again right away, even after her mother gets out of the hospital. It boiled down to: I was allowed to live with them. I didn't really want to before, but at this point I didn't want to at all.

It's just like he hasn't missed me one bit. He only wants to go away again.

So I decided to stay here. That was a relief, but then I started thinking about the new school and that I want to go to my own school, and it felt like my throat was in some kind of stranglehold. I just don't know. But I HAVE TO know. NOW!

I'm sick, that's all. (Isn't even really a lie.) Corry will just have to call. Which school is he supposed to call though?

later:
It was really nice yesterday when he was here, in spite of the fact that I felt weird the whole time because of the living situation and the school business.

I was so glad to see him, although at first I was shocked. He had a beard—even bigger than the one in those old pictures! He looked really awful! I almost couldn't look at him. The worst thing was that he didn't look like my dad anymore, even though he was. Later, I asked him why he had the thing. He said it had happened because of traveling. After a while it doesn't really matter to you how you look. It becomes unimportant. On top of that it's a big hassle, shaving. He gave his shaving gear away in Australia. That gave him a feeling of freedom, he said. From then on it was actually impossible to shave, so there was no need to anymore either.

"But now you're here," I said. "Now you can shave again."

"I've gotten used to it," he said. "I think it's okay like this."

"I think it's horrible," I said. "You don't look like my dad anymore."

He didn't like that. "What do I look like, then, if I don't look like your dad anymore?"

"You look like … a man with a beard."

He liked that. Thought it was funny, at any rate.

He drank beers with Corry (in the afternoon already!). I started cooking. When dinner was ready, he came out of the bathroom, without a beard (but with two Band-Aids)! He had shaved it off!

"I don't want to look like I'm not my son's father," he said.

I thought that was really awesome.

We talked. He told me a little about why he left. He wasn't himself anymore, he said. He had to go away to find himself again.

I asked whether he had found himself again now.

"That doesn't happen one-two-three," he said. "It takes time."

I don't understand a lot of it. How can you lose yourself? And where are you while you've lost yourself? Somewhere in India? In Memphis? Do you absolutely have to go all the way over there because that's where you *might* be?

"Losing yourself also happens very slowly," he said. "You don't even realize it. But once you realize it, then …" He looked at the floor, his voice got softer. "I thought it was awful to go and leave you behind." (Oh yeah? Didn't notice a thing.) "But I had to."

"But then why with Florrie?" I asked. "Why not alone?"

It was quiet for a time. "Hmm," he said. "Hmm."

"I just don't get it," I said. "I'd like to, though."

"I fell in love with her," he said. "Just like that, all of a sudden. I couldn't do anything about it. No, that's not true. I didn't *want* to do anything about it. Florrie was … she is …" He looked at me. He looked at Corry.

Corry asked him if he wanted another beer. He did. Corry disappeared into the kitchen.

"Let me put it this way…. No. Yes. It's just … No."

Corry came back with the beer. "Where's the neck flipper?" (Corry's word for bottle opener) "Oh, there it is." He flipped the caps off the longnecks (that's what he calls bottles of beer) and sat down again.

"She's very upbeat," said my dad. "Well, and a lot of other things besides. I fell in love."

"That can happen," said Corry. "Sometimes it just happens."

"Yes," said my dad. "But I think that Rits would like to know if … well, if that meant I didn't think his mother was fun to be with anymore. It's nasty when your parents split up, of course. At the time I just didn't know anything anymore. And I couldn't explain it."

"And now you can?" I asked.

"A little," he said. "I just couldn't take it anymore. I got more and more depressed. At first I didn't realize it. I was totally unhappy and didn't even realize it."

I don't get it. How can you be unhappy without realizing it? If you don't realize that you're unhappy, then you're *not* unhappy, right? So, I asked him how that could be.

"I didn't feel anything anymore," he said. "Everything was stuck. Jammed. Work. And everything. But yeah, what are you supposed to do? Looking back, I don't understand that for so long I ..." Suddenly he got up. "Need to go to the bathroom for a sec."

"But what are we supposed to do about school now?" I asked Corry.

"No idea."

"I have to go to school on Monday," I said to my dad when he finally came back from the bathroom. "I have to go to school, but I don't even have any school books or notebooks and I don't even know to which school I'm going. First I was going to go here, but now you're back."

"What do you want?" he asked.

"I want to go to my own school."

"So, you can come live with us, just for the time being."

As far as I know, I've never talked as long at one time with my dad as I did yesterday. I told him everything, about the movies, about The Geeks, about Rita and her mother and her father, and a lot more. It was fun. He really listened to everything. I know this because he said or asked something once in a while that made it obvious that he'd really listened. (For example: "But you'd also planned to be with The Geeks that day, hadn't you?" Or: "But how was that? Did Gerard know that Anneke was pregnant or didn't he, or did he think the baby was *his*?")

He didn't leave until it was really late, although just in time to catch the last train. He said he would drive back here and pick me up tomorrow night (meaning tonight). (He can borrow Florrie's mother's car because she doesn't need it now anyway.)

I'm not going though. I've decided that now. I don't want to live with Florrie. I'm staying here. Tomorrow I'll just go with Rita. I'll just see how things go with books and stuff there. I don't feel like getting worried about all that. I should have arranged it before, of course, the books and stuff, but first I didn't know where I was going to go to school, and once I knew, my dad was suddenly here and then I didn't know again.

I'm going to get up (and call my dad soon that I'm going to stay here a little longer anyway).

Monday, August 22

(Loose page, will stick it into the journal later)

It was the next to worst night of my life. (The worst one was that time with my mom, when it all went wrong and I had to go to Mrs. B's.)

I was just lying in bed and suddenly things started going wrong. I don't know why, I don't know how, but suddenly I felt like I was suffocating. Everything started spinning. I had stabbing pains everywhere. I thought I was dying. No, I was sure I was dying. Even Corry was in a panic. He wanted to call the hospital. No, no, not the hospital. If I was dying I didn't want to die in the hospital. I wanted to go to Dad. Corry first called him and then a cab. He went with me, onto the train as well. We got there in the middle of the night. My dad was waiting for me at the station. Everything was a blur. He grabbed me and brought me to a(nother) cab. I didn't see Corry again. I don't even know if he got back home that night or even if there was another train. I didn't even say good-bye.

And now I'm here, in another "cubbyhole." We're going to clean it up more and paint it and stuff.

This morning my dad called the schools to arrange all kinds of things. He's also making sure that it'll turn out all right with the books. This afternoon he picked up my class schedule. At first I wanted to go myself, but then I decided to stay here. Tomorrow, school starts for real and luckily I'll be there. Missing the first day of school is not cool.

First hour tomorrow, right away, is history with The Katie (Mrs. Ten Cate). Things are already starting off well. (That was *so* boring last year.)

Florrie said I wasn't dying but that I'd had a panic attack, hyperpipelation or something (something with "hype," I keep forgetting the term). She had had it herself once. It has something to do with breathing. She thought it happened because of everything that had been going on and my having to go to a new school on top of it all. It was because of the stress, she said.

I don't know. As far as I know, I started panicking only after the dizziness and the pain had already started, not the other way around.

Florrie's going to take me to the doctor so that he can reassure me. Other than that, hyperpipelation's not dangerous as far as she knows.

Sunday, August 28

I want to tape the loose sheet of paper into my journal but I can't find any tape. You'd think there would be tape somewhere in among all the piles of junk in this house, but no. Florrie said it had to be around somewhere, but she couldn't find it either.

At school everything's really normal, and therefore so weird. It's just like nothing happened. Steven had a whole lot of stories about France. We played soccer.

Took the train to see Corry yesterday. My dad wanted to bring me there with Florrie's mother's car, but I preferred to go alone. I picked up my things. I went over to Rita's. It was all really weird. It's still weird.

Corry and I sat in the living room.

"So," he said. "You're over there now."

"Yes," I said. "I'm over there."

"With your dad," he said. "That's good."

"Yeah."

"Yeah. Well, yeah, but for you it's good, I think."

"I think so."

"I'm maybe going to do some retraining," he said. "I'm going to be a repairman, of heaters and stuff like that."

"Cool."

"Your mother called twice. I told her you weren't home. You're going to have to tell her yourself."

"Yeah."

"So, you haven't told her anything yet?"

"No."

I brought the bike back to Pete. I said bye to Eva and Dachsy. (Alied wasn't home.) I told Pete I thought it was fun working with him. He said I was always welcome. I saw the cross and remembered I still hadn't asked about it, but this wasn't the moment to do that so I just let it go. He gave me a copy of the wedding video.

I went to Rita and Jaap's. Rita gave me her e-mail address. Said she'd keep me posted about the movie. We could make it together just the same, she said, if I wanted to. We arranged that I'll keep working on *The Making of Anneke* and that they'll do the takes of the rest of the family on the weekends so that I can come too.

Corry was happy with his present. He said he'd do his best to start using it. I told him it's not hard at all really.

He turned out to have a present for me too. It was a cookbook, nice and big, and very thick, with lots of pictures. That's a good thing, too, now that I've given him my *Tasty & Healthy*.

He took the bus with me to the train station. He shook my hand. He slapped me on the back. "Take good care of yourself," he said. "If something comes up, well … you know what."

"Yeah," I said.

Then my train came in.

later:

Florrie's pretty nice. Tuesday, when I was at school, she completely cleared out my cubbyhole so I can put some of my other things in there (as much as will fit). I can also use her computer. She came along to choose paint at the paint store too.

"I'm so glad that thing's gone," she said to me suddenly. She looked at my dad, who was studying a paint can farther down.

"What thing?"

"The beard. Horrible."

"Why didn't you ask him to shave it off?"

"I did quite a few times, but he flat-out refused."

I tried not to gloat too much.

Florrie painted all the walls yesterday when I wasn't there. It looks pretty cool now. Really small, but it's okay. It's only for a little while anyway.

Florrie's mother does have something bad. I don't know exactly what. I don't dare ask. They think that she'll get better again (but they don't know for sure).

I'm glad I'm here and going to my own school. That way at least something's still a bit normal, although I do miss everything *there*: Corry, Rita, Jaap, Eva, everybody. They suddenly seem really far away (which they are, obviously).

I got my pen back, by the way (the nice one I got for my birthday). It had been lost for a long time. My dad had it by accident as it turned out. He had found it in the pocket of a pair of pants while he was sorting clothes just before he went on his trip. He decided to take it with him. Cool, this pen's gone all over the world! He wrote my postcards with it too.

I told Florrie about it when we were washing the dishes. (I washed. She dried.)

"I know," she said. "That's what he said. 'Look, this is Rits's pen,' he said."

I asked whether she thought five postcards were a lot, in almost five months. Five postcards and zero phone calls.

"He thought of you all the time though," she said.

What good is it for somebody to be thinking of you all the time if you don't know that that person's thinking of you at all? Well, *now* I think it's pretty cool to know, but back *then* it did me no good.

"You should just talk with him sometime," she said. "Maybe then you'll understand it better."

"We already talked," I said.

"Maybe some more."

"Yeah. Maybe."

I don't know. I don't really feel like it, I don't think. I already had a practice conversation with him in my head. "Why did you send hardly any postcards? Why didn't you call?" I had asked. He gave very long, good answers and only said things I thought were nice to hear. (I came up with them myself, obviously.) I felt really good when it was over. I'm just going to forget about it for now. Am glad he's back.

I just remembered that I should call Tineke to tell her I'm here with my dad, but it's Sunday so she's not there.

I'm going to call my mom in a minute. It has to happen at some point.

later:
I called. I couldn't get her on the phone. She was busy doing

things, they said. She'd call me back. "Never mind," I said. Crap. Got myself all ready for the conversation and once again I can't talk with her.

later:

Suddenly I'd had enough. So I called again and said something like: she's my mother and I'm her son and it's very important and I'm going to keep calling again and again as long as it takes until I get her on the phone.

I could feel my heart going crazy as I was saying all that, but it worked! They went to get her. Getting her took a long time, but finally I had her on the phone.

She asked what was wrong. She sounded panicky.

I said there was nothing wrong, that I just wanted to talk with her, and that it was stupid that I could never speak with her when I called. She said she often had to do things there, be in consultation and therapy sessions and that kind of thing and that that was important.

I said that this was important too.

"What's wrong, then?"

"Dad's back."

Silence.

"Dad's back," I said. "Dad's back!"

"I can hear you."

"Then say something!"

She said nothing.

"I'm not at Corry's anymore," I said. "It's just for a little while, just that you know. I'm with Dad."

"Oh."

"And Florrie." This was the first time I spoke her name to my mom. It wasn't nice, but what was I supposed to do? THAT'S THE WAY IT IS!!! I can hardly pretend like it's not that way.

"Oh."

"I understand that you don't think it's nice, but that's just the way it is. I'm with Dad and Florrie. Until you're back again."

"I guess it's got to be. If that's how it is, then I guess it's got to be that way."

"That's the way it is."

I heard nose-snuffling and a couple of squeaks.

"Mom, cut it out," I said. "I can't do anything about it either."

I gave her the phone number. She said she didn't have a pen.

"I'm going to hang up," I said. "Corry has the number, I'm sure. Call him if you want it."

Then I hung up.

That's really weird. I actually feel pretty good. I hadn't been looking forward to telling her, but now that I'd done it, I felt a whole lot better than I expected.

I don't feel guilty or anything. I expected I would, but that's not how I feel.

Wednesday, August 31

I've already gotten seven e-mails from Rita (and sent eight). We'll see each other Saturday when she goes to interview an uncle. (I can't remember his name.) He doesn't even live very far away from here. I'm taking the train and she's going with Pete and Alied in the car. (For them it *is* far.) We'll all meet over there in front of the station.

Yesterday I played chess with my dad! He hadn't done it in years, but he won anyway (not as easily as Rita). I'm going to do it a lot, for as long as it takes until I'm really good—first better than he is, then better than Rita.

I write less and less. Had enough of it for a while, I think. Maybe I don't need to anymore. Maybe everything will be a little more normal now.

Thursday, September 1

I've got a cell phone! My dad said he understood that my mother would find it hard to call here. That's why he bought me a cell phone. Then she won't have to worry that she'll get Florrie or him on the line if she wants to call me.

I just called Corry to give him my cell phone number. If my mom calls him, he can give it to her. I don't really feel like calling her right now.

Corry asked how it was going.

"Fine," I said. "How're things with you?"

"Fine too," he said. "I've got a kind of a date. Well, not a real date. You know."

"With a woman?"

"Yes."

"A blind date?"

"No. She lives up the street here. I sometimes see her walking. She has two kids. We talked a little. And then she said like, 'Stop by for a cup of coffee sometime.'"

"Doesn't she have a husband?"

"No. Divorced, she said."

"No boyfriend either?"

"Not that I know of."

"Can she cook?"

"Don't know. But I cooked one time myself already. With your book."

Only once? "What did you make?" I asked.

"Navy bean casserole."

"Taste good?"

"Yeah, it stayed down pretty good."

I said that he should keep me posted. He said he would. After that, he said he was going to fix up the house.

"Good idea," I said. I asked if he'd cleaned up the *Angling and Anglers* already. He hadn't yet, but he was going to do it soon. He also said he had bought a new pair of trousers. Obviously one new pair wasn't enough. He hadn't gone to the same store though, because it was a dirty rip-off over there, he said.

I asked whether he'd bought new socks. He hadn't.